MASTER WANTED

RENT-A-DOM: BOOK 2

SUSI HAWKE
PIPER SCOTT

TROY

"*D*o you think you're clever, trying to trick me?"

Tonight, Master's tone was sharp and unyielding. I closed my eyes, my breath caught in my throat. Ice water trickled between my cupped fingers onto the leather seat of my office chair, then dribbled from its edge onto the wood floor—my punishment. I was to hold the ice against my balls until it was all gone. Throbbing cold seeped into my skin, and I wanted nothing more than to let the ice go, but I knew I deserved what I was getting. I'd been *bad*, and Master was well within his right to correct me.

It would only be a little bit longer. Just a little bit. Until then, I kept my bare legs spread as far as I could, one rested on my office desk, the other suspended over the arm of my chair.

Master spoke again. "Did you really think I wasn't going to notice?"

I bit down on my tongue, wanting to reply, but knowing better than to speak without explicit permission. I was already in trouble, and if I wanted my punishment to end, I was going to have to be good and mind my manners. Master's rules were as absolute now as they had been when we'd first connected a little more than a year and a half ago. I knew better than to defy them.

Tone every bit as rigid as it had been moments before, Master said, "I'm disappointed in you, Troy. You know what that means, don't you?"

Without a direct prompt, I wasn't allowed to speak—I wasn't allowed to make a noise—but the longer I held the ice to my body, the harder it got not to react to it. It was *cold*. Even when I squirmed and shifted in my seat, trying to relieve some of the burning chill that seemed to pulse beneath my skin, it wasn't enough to stop what I was feeling. There was nothing more than a thin sheet of it left now, but the few seconds it would take to melt would be torture. I bit down harder on my tongue, but despite my efforts, I whimpered.

"Oh, you know. Of course you know." Master hummed. "Has the ice melted yet? You may speak."

I released my tongue. The response burst from me. "Yes, Master, it's melted."

All that remained was the chill where it had been pressed against my balls and the remnants of water still pooled in the closed spaces between my fingers.

"Take a picture."

My heart raced. I glanced toward my office doors—luxurious seven-foot solid oak with semi-circular transom windows—and checked the locks. They were still in place. No one would make their way in.

"*Take a picture,*" Master demanded. "This is your last warning, Troy. You've already been bad once today. Do you want to test my patience?"

My phone was on my desk. I leaned forward, groping across the flat top with my dry hand until my fingers brushed against its corner. Desperately, I curled my fingers, dragging it toward me, then picked it up once it was within range. I tabbed out of the call with Master and toggled to the camera, snapping a quick picture of my dripping hand as it cupped my balls. As the picture sent, I took my hand away and took a picture of what lay beneath. When I saw the picture on the screen, a jolt of arousal seized me. My shaved balls were bright red where the ice had touched them, and my testicles were drawn so tightly to my body that they were almost nonexistent.

Seeing Master's will exerted like this on my body was a pleasure I seldom got to experience. With a choked moan, I sent the second picture. I wanted Master to see.

Master chuckled. "It looks like you're good for something tonight, after all. That's a very pretty color. I'd like to see it commemorated. What do you say? You may speak."

Hand trembling, I placed the phone back on my desk, screen down. The heavy rise and fall of my chest anchored me in the moment. The stinging pain of the ice cube against my skin was starting to recede. "Yes, Master."

"Good. Now..." Another hum. I sucked in a breath, trying to fill my lungs and curtail my excitement. Despite the torture Master had just put me through, I was hard. Aching. In need. To hear that I wasn't good enough was a reminder that Master expected more from me—wanted greatness from the man he'd chosen to dominate. As Master's possession, I had standards to meet, and god, did I want to meet them. No one but Master demanded I better myself. The yes-men in my inner circle wouldn't tell me no if I paid them to—but Master? He didn't give a shit about feeding my ego. He told it like it was, and he made sure I understood that he wasn't impressed by anything but the best.

And me?

I wanted him to deny me. Every "no" was an aphrodisiac, and I was desperate for my next taste.

My phone buzzed.

Master continued to speak. "Since you decided to use *my* bank account to fund whatever little pleasure purchase cost you three thousand dollars, you're going to use my money to get me something nice. Something to commemorate this moment. I've sent it to your phone. You'll buy it for me right now."

The bank account was mine, and so was the money in it, but I'd long ago surrendered control of it to my master. He controlled my personal finances, decided where my money was spent, and bought himself what he wanted, whenever he wanted it—to an extent. But hearing him now, demanding I spend money on him, pushing me to do it, make me forget that we had limits at all.

My erection throbbed. If I didn't bring myself under control, I'd come, and if Master found out...

Heart pounding to an erratic rhythm, I reached for my phone again and checked my conversation history with Master. Following the two previously sent pictures of my body was a hyperlink. I recognized the site—Master had sent me there before.

"You know what to do, don't you, Troy?" Master asked coolly. "If you waste my money by ordering the wrong size, we're going to have serious problems. You may speak."

"Yes, Master. I won't make another mistake." I tapped the link. The page loaded, and as the product image popped up on the screen, I had to suck in a breath. Master had linked me to tiny, cheeky lace panties, the same pretty red color the ice had left my balls. Red ribbons crisscrossed down the front like the laces on a corset. When Master slipped into them, the tight front panel and the lace that bound it would keep his cock snug. The red color against his skin would look sinful. When he turned while wearing them, the small back panel would only partially cover the curve of his ass.

Fuck.

Precum seeped from the slit of my cock. I fought orgasm.

"At just three hundred dollars, they're a fraction of what

you spent on yourself today," Master said. There was a bite to his tone that made me hunger to hear more. "Hand-crafted, designer, expertly assembled... tell me, did you get this kind of luxury out of whatever it is you spent that money on? Are you going to cherish it half as much as I cherish the *idea* of these panties? You may speak."

"No." I swallowed. A lump in my throat brought on from excitement made it difficult to speak, and my lust-fogged brain made assembling coherent sentences a struggle. "No, Master."

"I didn't think so." There was a moment of silence, then, "Click the button, Troy. Buy the panties for me. It's my money, isn't it? What are you waiting for?"

A juddering shiver worked its way up my spine. Precum oozed from my slit, trailing down my shaft to pool on my chilled balls. Unable to resist, I brought my water-wet hand to my cock and started to stroke slowly as my anticipation built. My free thumb hovered over the "buy now" button. All of my credentials were saved to the site, and my payment information was already on file...

One click and I'd give Master another small pleasure. One click and my time—my *life*—would materialize in this purchase and be given to the man who controlled my world.

"Troy?"

I tapped the button. My hand tightened around my dick, and I pumped furiously as the page went white and the loading bar at the top expended chunks at a time. When the confirmation page appeared, stating that my purchase had been received and would be shipped shortly, I let out a breath that was chased by a whine.

Master would wear my panties and embody my shame. Today's transgression would not be forgotten. Never.

"I got the confirmation email. Good boy, Troy. That wasn't so hard, was it?"

Another whimper. I was close. *So* close.

"But that was just round one. I've been keeping an eye on your accounts, you know, and I think that there's something else going on. Three thousand dollars isn't so much for you, is it? A drop in the bucket. A minute's worth of work. So what does that say about our budget? It's insulting, isn't it, that you'd give me such a small allowance each week? You can do better, Troy. You can do so much better. And so you're going to. I just took ten thousand dollars from the account. It's mine now. You're never going to see it again. And I'll be taking money regularly, whenever I want, to remind you that the money you make? None of it belongs to you. Every red cent is mine—just like you are."

Ten thousand dollars. According to our contractual agreement, Master was allowed to withdraw that much every three months, should he feel it necessary. He'd never abused the system before, and only ever used it to make a point. But for me, it wasn't about the money—the thrill of being denied paired with my need to provide, and it did wild and exciting things to my heart. Images bloomed in my mind, each more beautiful than the last.

Master, lounging in a hot tub at a spa, a flute of champagne suspended between his fingers, spending my money like it meant nothing to him—like I always had, and always would, be there to fund his extravagant lifestyle. Master, checked into a private suite, room service catering to him while he reclined in bed and texted me, showing me where my money had gone. Master, jetting first class to Europe, not having bothered to check his account before leaving, confident in the fact that my wealth would fund him no matter where he went, or what he did.

And if I had my way, it would.

As long as he kept telling me no, as long as he stayed strong, and confident, and fiercely independent, my account would be open for him forever. How many more times would he tell me no? How many more punishments would I suffer under his just command? So few people were brave enough to stand up to me, but Master hadn't once hesitated to show me my place.

God, did that do it for me. I would never want anyone else.

Excitement rocketed through me, its explosive pressure no longer willing to be held back. With a strangled cry, I came. Thick, pearlescent strands of cum striped the edge of my desk.

"If I were you, I'd keep an eye on your totals so you know how much you have on hand at any given time," Master said. "Now that our agreement has changed, you'll need to plan around fluctuations in available income. But with any luck, that'll light a fire under your ass, won't it? The more you make, the more padding you'll have for when I come to collect my share."

And the more you can take, I thought, already starting to get hard again. *The more you can bleed me dry...*

"Now that we've had our conversation about today's trespass, I'm done talking to you. Is there anything you have to say to me before I go? You may speak."

Like a diver breaching the surface of the water, I sucked air into my lungs and did my best to find the composure to speak. My mind, still cloudy from orgasm, struggled to put thoughts to words, but there was one question I always asked—one question my lips knew, and could navigate no matter the pressure I was under. "How much will it take so I can see you? How much... how much so we can meet?"

"Goodbye, Troy."

The call ended like it always did—with something only Master was brave enough to give me.

Denial.

And oh, *fuck*, did that turn me on.

2

ROBIN

My suitcase was royally fucked, and it wasn't about to get un-fucked any time soon. With a sigh, I rolled up my sleeves, broadened my stance sumo-wrestler style, then slammed down onto the top of the suitcase in a bid to compress it. I landed on the yawning flap, but the suitcase was so stuffed that it didn't make much of a difference.

Fuck.

"Are you having fun?" Monty asked. If I wasn't, *he* certainly was. There was a laugh in his voice, like he found my antics amusing.

"I'll have you know, since it seems like you've forgotten—" I gritted my teeth as I pushed against the flap of the suitcase with all my might, "—here in Rockport, suitcase wrestling is an official sport."

"Is that so?"

"Yes." I strained the word, slamming my elbow into the polyester. "It is."

"Well, isn't it a good thing you're coming back to Vegas, then?" Monty chuckled. I glanced at my laptop screen, but his video display was black—blocked out by the tape he kept over his webcam. "The sports we pursue here are much more... physical."

"Funny." I grasped the zipper and tugged. Reluctantly, the teeth started to click in place, and I kept pulling as hard as I could to keep the slider going. "You and the boys have been getting along fine without me. I'm not exactly a team player."

"But you are a player," Monty said. He always spoke with gravity, like every damned word out of his mouth was important. "Whether in Vegas or abroad, you're an important part of the team, Robin. It'll be good to have you home."

"Thanks." The suitcase finally closed all the way. The front bulged forward in unsightly ways, but it was a detail I could live with. As long as the bag didn't tip the scale at the airport, I was good to go. If the TSA wanted to search my bag, I wished them good fucking luck getting it zipped again. "You know, you can take the tape off your webcam when you talk to me, Monty. It's not like I'm going to be stealing company secrets."

"Not you, no... but I'd rather keep in the habit, thanks."

I sighed. Monty had always been a little paranoid—not that it was a bad thing—but it meant that for almost three years, I hadn't seen much of him.

"What are you going to do when I make it back to Vegas?" I asked. "Someone, sometime, somewhere is going to realize that something's up with us, you know?"

There was a moment's delay before Monty responded. I imagined him shrugging. "I'm not counting on it. The in-person meetings I hold are few and far between. Plus, I've taken measures to limit my presence."

"Like the tape," I said. I picked myself up from the suitcase and plucked a few times at my shirt, airing it out. The exertion to get the damned thing closed had left me sweaty and mildly sore. Fuck, did I need to get back into shape. Skinny and fit weren't synonymous.

"Like the tape," Monty agreed. "Don't worry yourself, Robin. It will be fine. You've been gone for so long and worked so hard that it's time to take a break. Come back to Vegas and let me take care of you."

I snorted. "You're starting to sound like my client."

"Perhaps. But there's a difference—"

"I know, I know." I wiped the sweat from my brow and shook my head. Monty would be able to see me through my webcam. "It's different now. Everything is. But I've done what I needed to do, and everything's going to be okay. I'll come spend some time with you in Vegas—you don't have to twist my arm—but if things start going south with Mom—"

"Then you're heading back to Rockport. I know." Monty's tone didn't change. "I'm not going to twist your arm into staying. I never would. What you're doing is..."

He didn't need to say it—we both knew what he meant. A profound feeling of sorrow clenched in my heart, and for a moment, I was silent.

"You can't be the hero all the time," Monty told me softly. "Right now, for your own mental health, it's important that you do something for you. Indulge in life while you're still young. You've done so much for me... if I can help you in that small regard, then it's the least I can do."

"I just feel so fucking greedy, you know?" I sat on the bed beside the suitcase, watching the blacked-out display on my laptop screen where Monty's face should have been. "I did what I did because I had to. Why should I be rewarded for it? People don't celebrate other people for doing the shit they need to do."

"You didn't need to do it."

"You know that's a lie." I sighed, letting it empty my chest and clear my head. "I've gotta hop on a plane in two hours, and you know what the drive to the airport is like."

"I won't keep you," Monty said. "I'll have a car waiting at the airport. The driver will be holding a sign for M. R. Would you like me to text you his details?"

"Please." I got up from the bed and pulled the suitcase down. Its plastic wheels clattered on the floor. "And if you haven't already seen to it, can you make sure that the pantry and fridge in my condo isn't empty? When I wake up tomorrow morning, I'm going to hate my life if there isn't coffee and creamer."

"Of course."

I made sure the suitcase was balanced on its wheels, then moved to the computer. In its black display, I saw my reflection. Dark, messy hair, slender, elegant angles, and worried eyes. Shit. Monty was right—I could use some time off.

"I'll see you a little later," I told him, setting a hand on top of the screen. "Don't do anything I wouldn't do."

Monty chuckled. "I don't think we'll have a problem. Be safe."

"Always am." I winked.

"You've got your wallet?" Mom asked.

I glanced at her from the corner of my eye, noticing the way her pixie-cut short dark hair whipped in the wind. Her window was cracked open as we raced down the highway, and the whoosh of moving air was almost deafening.

"I've got my wallet, Mom," I promised.

"And your phone?" she pressed. "You'll need your phone so your brother can get in touch with you."

"I've got my phone."

"And your carry-on?" Her fingers tightened around the hand grip on the door, like she was afraid I might remember I'd forgotten something and make a U-turn on the interstate to go reclaim it. "Do you have your liquids packed in your check-in luggage? Because they don't let you take them through security anymore. You don't want to be pulled aside."

"Mom," I said with a laugh. I rolled up the window with a press of the door button, cutting out the noise of the wind so we could talk more easily. "It's okay. I've got it handled. This isn't my first flight. I promise, I'll be okay."

My reassurance didn't placate her. "I'm your mother. I worry. It's my job."

"And my job is to make you worry as much as possible, I'm sure." Traffic grew thicker and started to back up. I slowed accordingly. The airport wasn't far. "But, I'll have you know that I've made it out the last few years of my life unscathed, all kinds of travel included. The only person you need to worry about is yourself."

She made a non-committal noise.

"If it bothers you, I'll stay," I told her. "You were the one pushing me to get out of the house for a while, but I'd gladly turn around and drive back to Rockport with you if you feel you're not ready to do this on your own."

"Don't you dare." The worry in her voice turned to

staunch refusal. She crossed her arms over her chest. "After everything you've done, you deserve to have some fun and live your own life. You can't stay cooped up at home forever. There's so much more waiting for you out there than what Rockport can offer you." She pushed her fingers through her hair, trying to brush it back into some semblance of neatness. These days, it was looking more thin and brittle than it ever had before, but Mom had never been the kind to wear wigs. "Besides, if you don't go, who will look after Monty for me? It's been three years, and they don't call it Sin City for nothing."

I almost choked trying to hold back my laughter. Oh, god. If only she knew...

"Mom?" I asked. "You're aware Monty isn't eight anymore, right? He's an adult now. I'm not going to be policing his 'sleepovers.'"

I only caught Mom's expression from the corner of my eye, but I was pretty sure she was holding back laughter, too. "Oh, I know. I didn't mean sex, Robin. Sex is a wonderful, beautiful thing if it's shared between two or more consenting adults."

"Or more?" My cheeks went red. "Oh my god, Mom..."

"What?" I was pretty sure she was trying to embarrass me

on purpose at this point. "There's nothing wrong with having more than one partner as long as you're crystal clear with everyone involved what's going on. In fact, your father and I—"

"Oh my god," I squeaked. I liked to think of myself as a pretty open-minded individual—casual sex, multiple partners, toys, kink... all of it was fine by me. Even if I wasn't into it, most of the time, I could understand the appeal. But hearing my mom talk about her sexual adventures with Dad? That was something I *couldn't* handle. "Mom, I love you, but I need you to stop talking right now. You probably don't want to keep teasing the son who's driving a ton-and-a-half deathtrap at sixty in heavy traffic."

"Well then, I'll cut it short." She returned a hand to the grip on the door. "Sex isn't a sin, and I don't want you to police it. What I want to make sure of is that you keep Monty on the straight and narrow—don't let him get involved in the darker side of the city. That's not something I want for either of you. Can you do that for me?"

"Mom..." Guilt raked its fingernails down the back of my skull. I spared her another glance before locking my eyes on the road again. If sex wasn't a sin, then what did we have to worry about? Monty's business was aboveboard. He reported his income and paid taxes, just like anyone else. Nothing shady was going on—both of us had too much to lose to let illegal practices shut us down. "I'll make sure to keep an eye on him, okay?"

"Good boy."

I sighed.

"And," she added, "just to let you know, if I find out you and Monty have been misbehaving out there in Vegas, you can expect me on the next plane so I can come smack you both upside the head."

"I believe it, Mom." The turnoff for the airport was coming. I checked over my shoulder, then merged into the indicated lane. "Trust me, neither of us are looking to be *that* bad."

"That's good." I heard the mischief in her voice. "Because if you were, then I'd have no choice but to supplement the smackdown you'd receive with a few things your father taught me about tying someone up, when we were young and f—"

"Whoa, whoa, whoa! What did I say about the ton-and-a-half deathtrap?" Fuck. At least I knew where I got it from. "Let's talk about something that isn't likely to make me veer into the guardrail. Can you ask me if I remembered to charge my phone before I left the house?"

"*Did* you remember to charge your phone?" Mom asked pointedly, as though our previous conversation had never happened.

That was better. I laughed. "Yes, Mom, I did."

It was a good thing I'd charged it, too. I had a certain delinquent casino owner to check up on.

And expensive, in-air purchases to make on a certain someone's dime.

3

TROY

*S*hortly after three in the afternoon, a frantic knock at my door distracted me from my paperwork. I closed my laptop, then rose from my desk. There were only a handful of people who had unimpeded access to my office—the upper executives under my employ and my personal secretary, Lena—so it came as no surprise when I pulled open the door to find Eugene Westward standing on the other side.

Eugene was balding. A crown of wispy black hair sprouted from the sides of his head, but the top had receded year by year until it had vanished completely. From time to time, Eugene combed his wispy hairs over his massive bald spot in what I believed was an attempt to conceal the fact that his problem had advanced beyond the point of no return, but today was not one of those days. Today, his hair stuck out from either side of his head, but was flattened at the back, like he'd been tugging at it in frustration all morning.

He may have been a touch balder than the last time I'd seen him. It was hard to tell.

"Sir?" Westward asked timidly. He folded his fingers together and glanced at his shoes, but didn't dare come into my office. "Hello, sir. I'm, um, I'm sorry to bother you, but it's important—*imperative*—that we have a conversation. Whatever you're working on, no matter how pressing it is, needs to wait."

Nothing I'd been working on was pressing. I took a step back from the doorway and looked Westward over, a repressed laugh tugging at the corner of my lips. Westward had been with me since before I'd taken over The Palisade from my father, and he'd served as my executive adviser since. To this day, he was the same, pudgy, bumbling man I'd gotten to know while learning how to run the family business—nervous, anxious, but entirely reliable.

"Come inside, Westward," I said. I gestured into the room, but kept a hand on the door. "If whatever you have to say is that important, then we shouldn't have the conversation out in the hallway."

"No, certainly not." Westward scurried inside. He moved just as frantically as he spoke. "Really, you should be sitting down for this, so it's best we go speak at your desk. I'd like you to be comfortable, please."

I arched a brow. "Is that so?"

"Yes. Very, very much so." Westward plucked at his sleeves, toying nervously with the buttons of his cuffs. A thin sheen of perspiration glistened on his brow, and his cheeks were red. His pasty skin contrasted with the bold color and made his beady blue eyes pop. "It really is advisable that you... that you sit down for this. It's in your best interest."

Well, that was new. Most of the time, when Westward came to tell me the sky was falling, he rushed through a long-winded explanation as soon as the door was closed. It wasn't like him to hold back on potentially world-ending information.

Tantalized by the change, and rather amused by his behavior, I crossed my arms loosely over my chest and cocked my head to the side. "Well, Westward, I'll have you know that I've had enough sitting for today. Why don't you tell me while I'm standing? It'll be good for my circulation."

Westward let out a panicked breath through his nostrils, whistling like a tea kettle. "Sir..."

The laugh I'd been holding back arrived, and no amount of biting my tongue could stop it. I truncated it into one crisp bark, then shook my head. "If I pass out and break my skull while falling, I won't hold you accountable. If you've got a medical release form, I'll sign it."

"Sir," Westward said, exasperated. "Really..."

"Go ahead. What's the trouble-du-jour?" I anticipated more of the same old. Some upheaval in the staff—maybe a lost contract with a client. If we lost our cleaning company, Pressed 4 Time, it would throw a serious wrench in our hotel operations. It wouldn't surprise me if that was exactly what had happened. "I'm ready."

"There's been an incident, sir," Westward murmured. He glanced aside, then shook his head like a dog fresh out of the bath. Whatever was causing him so much grief had to be bad if he needed to power through his anxiety like that. I'd worked with Westward long enough to know that, for as nervous as he always was, he wasn't often twitchy. "It's about Donovan Redding, sir."

"Redding?" I narrowed my eyes, trying to piece together what Westward was going on about. For the last five years, Redding had been my director of facilities—one of the men instrumental in assuring the casino's quarterly goals were met by overseeing interior operations. Amongst other things, he was responsible for plans, budgeting, and scheduling modifications to the casino and its staff structure. "He's been sick for the last few days—he hasn't gotten worse, has he? Is everything okay?"

"No, that's not it." Westward sighed nervously. He wrung his hands. "Mr. Redding didn't come in for work today, either, but Ms. Afia needed to get in touch with him regarding a... a..." Westward shook his head again, then tugged at his hair nervously and continued. His glasses were crooked, but he didn't seem to notice. "It doesn't matter. Ms. Afia needed to get in touch with him, so she called his cell phone, figuring she'd leave a message if he didn't pick up, just like every other time we've tried. Only this time, the number was disconnected."

"What?" I frowned. "Disconnected?"

"It was... very strange," Westward agreed. "No one quite knew what to do about it. But Ms. Afia is very perceptive, and she got in touch with HR, who placed a call to his other number on file. It was disconnected, too."

"There must be some mistake," I said. "Why would Redding's numbers be disconnected? There must be an issue with his service provider. Doesn't he have a company phone?"

"That's the thing, sir..." Westward sighed nervously. He couldn't stop wringing his hands. "The only phone still connected was Redding's work phone, which we discovered sitting on his empty desk. Empty, as in... the desk was vacated. Stripped down. The room had been gutted. It was like Redding had never been there at all."

"Westward, you're making me feel like I've stepped into the *Twilight Zone*." I glanced at my closed office doors, glad that I'd dragged him inside. I was beginning to regret not taking Westward's advice to sit. The conversation was unsettling enough as it was, and I knew the other shoe was about to drop. "What's going on with Redding?"

Westward sucked in a breath, lips rounded like a fish hauled out of water. "The short of it is... Mr. Redding has been embezzling money from The Palisade since his first year of employment, and we suspect that he's fled the country, likely to Southeast Asia."

Westward might as well have slapped me full-force for the effect those words had on me. For a moment, I was breathless, too stunned to speak. Then, as I gathered my resources, I asked the question I dreaded the most. "How much has he embezzled?"

"It's... it's too early to tell for certain," Westward mumbled. "But... early reports predict probably... probably in the tens of millions, sir. He was sending money to a fraudulent vendor of his own design—a cleaning company the hotel had allegedly been sending its linens to, Pressed 4 Time. As it turns out, there were two companies listed who took care of the hotel's washing... but only one of them was real. Mr. Redding... claimed those expenses as taxable deductions to remove them from Palisade profits, then provided falsified receipts for them, which he submitted to the accounting department without issue. Everything appeared to be above the board by the books. Until Ms. Afia demanded an investigation, there were no red flags at all."

Time slowed. Syllables blurred. I stared at Westward as dread crumpled my stomach and the tremendous pressure of an unbearable burden settled on my shoulders. Tens of millions of dollars gone, falsified reports sent to the IRS as factual and true, and expenses the casino had claimed, but could no longer prove...

Redding hadn't only screwed me—he'd fucked me over, taken pictures of the mess, then posted them online for the whole world to see. If we were audited—and after this, I knew it was only a matter of time—what was I going to do? Depending on how much Redding had spirited away with, I'd owe tens of millions in back taxes on his tens of millions of dollars stolen, and that was money we'd never see.

Not a dollar of it.

Because if Redding had fled the country and gone to Southeast Asia with that kind of cash? There was no way that he was ever setting foot on US soil again. He'd spend the rest of his days slung up in a hammock by the ocean, waited on hand and foot by locals he'd keep on his private payroll. He'd shed his identity like a snake sheds its skin and start life over as Pete, or Hank, or Bill. And he'd do it all on money stolen from me.

Money that should have belonged to Master.

The dread in my stomach tightened. Pressure pushed at my skull, and black dots appeared before my eyes.

What was Master going to think of this? Tens of millions of dollars, gone. Money he'd never known existed. Money *I'd* never known existed.

Money that was going to affect my bottom dollar, now that I knew about it.

"Do you need to sit down, sir?" Westward asked. He continued to wring his hands. If he didn't stop, he was going to twist them off at the wrist. "I asked if you would, but you... you were insistent, so..."

"Westward," I said, my voice thin. "I don't need to sit down. I need you to get me a bottle of bourbon—any kind will do—and then I need you to get out of my office so that I can figure out what the hell I'm going to do."

"Would you like a glass, sir?" Westward stumbled over his feet on the way to the door.

I glared at him. He got the message.

"R-right away, sir," Westward promised. "It'll be... be just a few minutes. I'll take care of it immediately."

"Thank you."

I watched as Westward attempted several times to push the door open, using more and more force, until, desperately, he realized his folly and yanked the door open. He scurried out the door, then slammed it accidentally. From behind the oak, I heard him shout, "Sorry, sir!" before there was total silence.

He was gone.

Once I had silence, I counted down from ten to give Westward ample time to distance himself from the door, then lifted a hand to my mouth and held it there, like if I could keep my scream contained, my problem would disappear.

My accounting team would work out a solution. They would find a way to tweak our disbursements to recover the money we'd need to pay when we adjusted the last five years of taxes. What bothered me wasn't the threat of financial ruin—the twisting feeling in my gut was brought on by two distinct feelings, each of them unmistakable.

First was the profound sense of violation—someone I trusted had stolen from me, stabbing me in the back in the process.

The second, and the one I kept coming back to time and time again, was how upset Master would be that I'd allowed such a trespass to happen. When he found out—and he would, even if I tried to keep it hidden from him—I'd be in shit. Deep, deep shit.

Multiple millions lost in the blink of an eye. Money I hadn't even known I had.

Master was going to kill me. All the bourbon in the world wouldn't save me from that.

4

ROBIN

nce upon a time, when my heart had been torn to pieces with worry and I'd felt like I couldn't go on, my brother Monty had sent me an email with three attachments—"The Rules.docx," a contract, and a blank template for a personal profile. *Give it a read, Robin,* he'd written. *Tell me what you think. I know that you're burned out after caring for Mom, but if you have the inclination, I think I may have found the perfect client for you...*

Previously, I'd told Monty that I wasn't interested in taking on contract work for his company, Rent-a-Dom— that I was too busy caring for Mom and making weekend trips to unsuspecting casinos to dominate some alpha who wouldn't remember me in a week's time. The payout wasn't worth it when I could spend a weekend counting cards and come out thousands of dollars richer, but Monty had changed my mind with a single sentence.

The client is Troy Sullivan.

Troy Sullivan, the hotshot casino mogul who'd threatened to "throw my ass in jail" if he saw me on his property again. The one who'd had me detained in the pit and dragged up to his private office like a petty thief so he could tell me what a lowlife I was for counting cards and stealing his precious money. His face, eyes narrowed with anger and lips curled in disgust, stuck in my memory. Of all the casinos I'd been banned from, and of all the encounters with casino personnel I'd endured, his was the one I'd never forget. Card counters in Vegas were a dime a dozen, but for whatever reason, he'd singled me out and brought me up to see him when I should have simply been escorted off the premises. He'd humiliated me when what I needed most was compassion.

If Troy Sullivan was my client, I was all in.

I'd filled out the personal profile, signed the contract, and perused the rules to refresh my memory while tucked into a lavish hotel room bed in Atlantic City. A year before, I'd written those same rules with Monty while he got his company off the ground—we'd both been going to business school at the time, and had moved to Vegas from our small hometown in Maine so we could simultaneously launch Monty's startup, Rent-a-Dom. Originally, both of us were going to have equal shares in the company, but after Mom had gotten sick, I'd signed over all rights to him so I could take care of her while Monty stayed behind and built his empire. I'd been gone for so long that I only had vague recollections of what we'd decided was necessary, but as I familiarized myself, I was glad to see it was as simple and straightforward as I'd remembered.

A sexual content disclaimer—boring. Mandatory STD and background checks—*yawn*. The Dom can refuse a client if he or she desires—standard.

I'd abide by the rules down to the letter if it meant I'd be able to sink my claws into that man.

To think that I'd be bringing him to his knees? To think that I'd be the one calling the shots, and the one bending him to my will?

It had seemed too good to be true.

But it wasn't.

Troy, intrigued by my blank profile picture and the single letter I'd submitted as my name—R—had signed on for a month-long package with me through Rent-a-Dom. That was all it had taken to make him mine. The next year and a half, he'd come back time and time again, paying any premium I'd demanded for a sliver of my time. What had started as a way to get revenge by making a profit off the man I despised the most had turned into something else—something cathartic. I'd never admit it out loud, but I'd found pleasure in dominating Troy.

I'd been hired to tell him no, but these days, it was getting more and more tempting to say yes.

AT FORTY THOUSAND FEET, curled up in my extra-wide seat, I saw an excellent opportunity to remind Troy of what he couldn't have.

Look at where I am, I wrote. Languidly, I tapped the camera icon and took a shot of my small, private cabin, with just my slippered feet in the shot. It was separated from the other first-class seats by a curtain, ensuring me at least a little privacy. I curled my toes against the plush bottoms of my slippers and inspected the picture to make sure there were no incriminating details in it, then sent it and its accompanying text off.

Troy saw the text almost immediately and started to type. I grinned.

Is it comfortable, Master?

Very. I raked my teeth across my lip, debating how to proceed. In the year and a half since Monty had matched me to Troy, I'd learned what he liked best about being financially dominated, and what didn't work for him. It was my job to keep him happy, and sometimes, that meant going about our business in unusual ways. *But why don't you make it comfier? Tell me about how much money I earned today.*

The reply was delayed. That in itself wasn't unusual—most times, Troy double-checked figures before sending them to me. It was better that he was accurate than quick. He'd been punished more than once for having reported a faulty figure. I wouldn't stand for sloppiness. A man like him needed to exercise caution in everything he did. A single botched number on a report could mean a loss in the hundreds of thousands, and while I wasn't the IRS, I sure as hell was as capable of putting his balls in as tight of a vise as they were... and most times, I thoroughly enjoyed doing so.

But as the minutes ticked by and Troy failed to respond, I knew that something was up. Behavior like that wasn't typical of him. I'd been gone all of a day while I got ready for my flight, and he'd gone and fucked things up already.

The man was the least professional successful business owner I'd ever had the displeasure to meet.

He had to be doing it on purpose. There were times when Troy craved punishment more than he wanted to be rewarded. Why else wouldn't he answer?

Give me an answer, Troy.

I was no stranger to how much money Troy's casino made —and how much more money it could be making, if only Troy pulled his head out of his ass and restructured management. From time to time, when the mood was right, I played dumb and acted like I had no clue, but we both knew better. Troy got a kick out of roleplaying, and if the client was happy, then I was doing my job. Today, however, with Troy beating around the bush, wasn't one of those days.

Profits are down today, Troy finally admitted. *Very down.*

Explain.

It was discovered today that one of the men on my executive team has been embezzling money from the casino—using a cleaning company as a front to write off millions of dollars over the years that he pocketed.

Disbelief narrowed my eyes, and I sent back a single word. *What?*

No one suspected a thing, Troy continued. I imagined his face tight with disappointment and worry, his thumbs flying across the screen of his phone as he composed his reply. *One day the guilty party was here, the next he was gone. He's disconnected his phones, gutted his office, abandoned his condo, and likely taken off for another country. Accounting is going over the records, combing the figures for suspicious activity so we can tabulate a total number... but it's not looking good.*

Fuck.

I scrubbed at my face, then looked away from the screen of the phone to the curtain separating me from the rest of the cabin. What I wanted was to call Troy up through my Wi-Fi connection so I could judge the tone of his voice and determine what he needed most from me right now, but the curtain wouldn't keep our conversation private. While some travelers were happy to talk sensitive business throughout a flight, I was more sensible than that—Troy's screw-up needed to stay between us. I had no choice but to keep texting.

The fact that Troy had responded to me at all meant that he was looking for comfort—for someone else to take the responsibility off his shoulders, even for a little. While I hated what the man had done to me, we'd spent too long together for me to feel nothing for his plight. If he needed me to dominate him, then I'd dominate the *shit* out of him.

And maybe, maybe...

An idea started to percolate in my mind, but I stored it away for later consideration.

I'm disappointed in you, Troy. It was a simple statement, but one I hoped would set the tone of what was to follow. If Troy didn't want to be punished for his lack of foresight, then he could end the conversation before it got any more intense.

I know, Master. I'm sorry.

Tone was hard to discern through text, so I had to trust that Troy would be honest and tell me if he'd had enough. The fact that he hadn't gently asked that I back off gave me the clearance I needed to push harder.

You know that you'll be punished for this, don't you?

Yes, Master.

I reclined in my seat and lifted the phone up, as if changing the angle of the screen could give me a new perspective on the situation. Even though Troy wanted for nothing, a loss in the millions was emotionally devastating. It was the kind of violation a man didn't just shrug off.

How many times have I told you to have another set of eyes comb over the figures, Troy? I realized after sending the message that my hands were shaking. It wasn't because I was particularly invested in Troy's success—if his casino crashed and burned tomorrow, I'd move on—but because, when I tapped into my Dom headspace, it was hard *not* to feel like I wasn't directly involved.

I'm sorry, Master.

Sorry isn't good enough. Give me percentages. How much is this impacting your business?

We have to go over years of reports. The figures are steep. Early estimates predict between ten to fifteen percent of last year's revenue is lost... and if the IRS audits us...

Double fuck.

I am very disappointed, I replied. *Very, very disappointed. What is your plan?*

I have my accounting division working overtime while I'm restructuring hotel management, looking for new employees with experience in reporting to take over while this mess gets sorted out.

No. I clenched my teeth. *What is your plan to make it up to me?*

Troy started and stopped typing several times. Then came the response.

I don't know, Master. I don't know how I can tell you how sorry I am.

I let a steady breath out through my nose, then let the calm, zen-like power that dominance brought me wash through my body, pushing out the negativity. Every action had an equal and opposite reaction, and Troy was about to learn that firsthand.

Of course you don't have an idea, I wrote. *You have no idea how to take care of yourself, do you, pet? That's okay. I'll teach you.*

What do you mean, Master?

I glanced at the time as it was displayed on the top right corner of my phone, then pursed my lips and replied. *Don't let it bother you. You'll find out soon enough.*

5

ROBIN

*M*onty's driver waited for me by the baggage carousel, dressed in a pressed suit and jacket, his lips a line and his eyes set dead ahead right until the point where I came to stand in front of him, when he deigned to look at me. His white hair was kept short, close to buzzed. Like Monty had said he would be, he was in possession of a printed sign that simply read "M. R."

"Hello, sir," the driver said cordially.

"Hey." I paused. "I'm the M. R. you're looking for, but there's been a change of plans."

He blinked and said nothing, but the pale blues of his eyes scrutinized me.

I gave him a second to get over himself, then continued. "I have a few errands I need to take care of before I head back to my condo, so I'll be arranging my own transportation. I'd appreciate it if you could deliver my bag, though. I don't want to have to worry about it while I'm out."

"Of course, sir." The driver's voice was monotonous, but I could tell from the expression on his face that he was so over me. "Before I deliver the bag, is there anything you need from inside of it?"

"I've already taken out everything I need," I replied. "Fair warning: it's pretty heavy. Let me wheel it to the car for you. I can at least get it loaded in the trunk."

The driver's eyes remained fixed on me, but I wasn't sure he was seeing me. After however long he'd been serving Monty, I supposed I couldn't blame him—he'd probably had to learn pretty quickly how to tune everything out. I could only imagine the things that went on in my brother's home. "Unnecessary, sir. I'll be happy to bring it to the car myself."

"I insist." I glanced toward the doors leading out of the airport. The sun had set, and bright lights chased away the darkness. "I've got a long night ahead of me, and a little exercise will help get me fired up. Take me to where you're parked?"

The driver barely masked his dreary sigh. "Yes, sir."

What a party animal.

We left the airport and headed for the designated parking area, my luggage clicking behind me.

It was going to be one hell of a long day, but what I had planned? It was going to make it more than worth it.

THE PALISADE HOTEL and Casino occupied a prominent spot on the Strip, its thirty-eight floors lit up from the outside by spotlights, its wavelike, cascading architecture impressive and vaguely reminiscent of the buildings I'd seen in downtown Chicago. Its facade was inlaid with tiny crystals invisible to the naked eye, but that sparkled in the floodlights, making The Palisade shine like a diamond. Travel sites had taken to calling it "The Gem of the Las Vegas Strip," and at night, it wasn't hard to tell why.

Spanning The Palisade's exterior courtyard was a vast fountain. A column of transparent oversized gemstones of different sizes and cuts were stacked at its center, lit up from the inside. Water gushed from the top and poured over the sides, running along the gems' smooth faces and streaming from suspended corners. Instead of pennies, the bottom of the fountain was layered with gemstone after gemstone, each of them installed to prevent thieving hands from carrying them away. It didn't stop tourists from trying—they sat in clusters at the sides of the fountain, hands in the water, picking and prying.

I didn't have the heart to tell them they were coveting cubic zirconia at best.

I cut around the fountain and headed for The Palisade's front doors. Three sets of steps divided it from the courtyard, two broad ramps on either side offering accessibility for all patrons. I took the steps at a jog, then rolled my shoulders back as I stepped through the doors. The lobby area was accessible to the public, and while there was security in place to make sure none of The Palisade's guests were jostled or panhandled, no one was there to stop me from entering the premises. From what I knew of Troy and the quality of most of his employees, I suspected it would be a while before anyone clued in that Robin Mills had infiltrated the building.

I took a left from the lobby, heading through the lavishly decorated archway leading into the casino. A bouncer stood on either side of the doorway, and both looked my way when I passed, but neither said anything or tried to stop me. If I hadn't known The Palisade as well as I did, it would have surprised me—I was twenty-two, but barely looked it—but I knew that the staff here was inattentive at best. No one was going to say or do jack shit until it was too late.

I slipped my hands into the pockets of my black slacks and made my way to the cage. Years ago, when Mom's health had deteriorated, I'd put my mind to use and toured casino to casino counting cards, cashing out large dollar sums every night, never hitting the same place twice, and always playing by the rules. By federal law, casinos were required to alert the IRS to any player who cashed out over ten thousand dollars on any given night, but beyond federal law, there were casino rules that limited and complicated winnings. Some places wouldn't allow a player to hold onto any winning chips valued one hundred dollars or more after a winning hand—they had to be cashed out immediately, oftentimes involving a phone call from the cage to the pit to verify the chips had been legally obtained. Some places demanded ID at different thresholds of earning—most often three thousand dollars—and tracked undesirable players that way, declining them service when those players became "too good for the game." Casino hopping and card counting wasn't only about being smart about the cards left in play and the probability of a particular number being pulled, but about the research behind every establishment and its quirks. If I could milk a casino out of three thousand dollars a night for a week before I was banned, it was better than a singular payday that skirted the ten-thousand-dollar mark but alerted everyone and their uncle that I was far from the typical player.

Tonight, though, I wasn't looking to be discreet. Tonight, I *wanted* eyes on me.

I leaned against the counter and spoke to the woman on the other side of the glass, putting on my best sly smile as I slid my debit card into the payment slot. "Ten thousand in Barneys."

The woman looked at me. While she did her best to remain casual, a glint of suspicion shone in her eyes. She performed the transaction, but I knew from that single look that security would be keeping a close eye on me. How long would it take them to figure out who I was?

The cashier placed my poker chips—worth five hundred dollars each and colored purple like their eponymous dinosaur—in the slot and pushed them to me. With them in my possession, I left the cage and headed for the pit. If I'd wanted to blow my cover right away, I would have paid admission to the high roller area, but the idea of really twisting the knife appealed to me more, so I settled for a more discreet approach.

I slotted into the first blackjack table I could find and laid down my chip. The dealer's eyes shot to mine, shocked, and I offered her a pleasant smile. With five hundred dollars on the line, I was in the game and back in action. Step one of tonight's master plan: complete.

6

TROY

The worst day in my life over the past few years ended with me home alone, in bed in the dark, too frustrated to sleep. All the little details I'd tried to shunt out of my mind swarmed back to me, a thousand annoying gnats all vying for my attention. I closed my eyes tightly and clenched my fists, trying to force them out of my head, but the harder I pushed, the faster they came back.

Millions of dollars, gone.

Trouble with the IRS.

An audit.

Master, audibly displeased.

A mysterious punishment I couldn't begin to anticipate.

A personal betrayal.

Goddamn Donovan Redding, laughing himself silly in a hammock in Cambodia.

What the hell was I going to do? All of my problems kept stacking, each adding more pressure than the last, until it felt impossible to knock them down. I had to do something, but I couldn't figure out the best place to start. All I wanted to do was close my eyes, hold my phone up to my ear, and let my master take control. When he was in charge, I didn't have to worry about the crushing issues of my day-to-day life. All I had to worry about was respecting his word and being *good*.

Master...

I closed my eyes and let my thoughts drift back to our last correspondence. There'd been anger in Master's voice, certainly, but I'd heard something else, too. Fear? Regret? Sympathy? Whatever it was, it was soft and vulnerable, and it made me feel worse than if Master had only been angry with me.

What good was I if I couldn't even make the man who mattered to me happy?

I scrunched my nose, my eyes still closed, and rolled onto my side. My sheets glided against my bare skin. I was stripped down to my boxer-briefs, my suit hung to be dry cleaned tomorrow.

If Master really was upset over what I'd lost, how could I make it up to him? When the audit was over and life returned to normal, I knew I'd be turning a profit again, but the money wasn't what mattered—not really. Master had warned me to be careful with how I did business. He'd called me inattentive and foolish to have made the choices I had, and to have structured my staff so poorly. At the time, I'd been too arrogant and sure of myself to pay attention, but now I knew better. He'd been right. I needed to change the way my business was structured if I wanted to prove to him I was truly sorry.

But how?

Minutes ticked by, bleeding into hours. I didn't know how long exactly it had been, but I was finally falling asleep when an echoing knock sounded on my bedroom door. I jumped and sat upright, then rubbed the sleep from my eyes and reached for my bedside lamp. With a click of its switch, a halo of light engulfed my bed, nightstand, and the surrounding floor. It was enough to see by.

"Come in," I said.

The doorknob twisted and the door opened, allowing one of my personal bodyguards—Damien—to enter. He bowed his head politely, then spoke. "Sir... we have a problem."

Another problem? I was getting too old for this shit. With a lengthy sigh, I combed a hand through my hair and braced myself for the worst. Damien was highly capable, and the entire time he'd been under my employment, he'd never had to come to me with a problem before. If it was serious enough to warrant waking me up in the middle of the night, it had to be something important. "What kind of problem are we talking about, Damien?"

"There's an issue at The Palisade." Damien cut right to the chase, refusing to mince his words. Over the last few months, I'd remarked a change in him. At first, I'd been inclined to pin it on grief, as he'd just suffered the unexpected loss of a long-time friend, but grief didn't energize a man or put the spark back in his eyes. Damien was sharper and more observant than he'd ever been before. If he kept it up, he was looking at a sizable raise. "Security has uncovered an undesirable player. He's maxed out all the boxes on one of our blackjack tables... and he's winning."

"Why is this a concern of mine, and not an issue security's

already dealt with?" I asked. Undesirable players cut into profits and needed to be regularly weeded from the casino, but it was no reason to wake me up in the middle of the night. The security team should have escorted him out and banned him from the premises already. The last time I'd confronted a card counter face-to-face had been years ago—and that was because the kid had been underage and had *still* cleared me out of close to fifty thousand dollars over the course of two weeks. I figured I could scare him straight and stop him from heading down a destructive path. At the end of the day, gambling was gambling, and he was setting himself up to lose.

"He..." Damien paused. "He's been there a little more than fifteen minutes, and he's already won a hundred thousand dollars."

I paused. Blinked. Processed.

"We've got the cameras on him," Damien explained. "The pit boss is keeping an eye on things, too. We don't see any devices. Security thinks he's counting, but they can't pinpoint his technique. All they can agree on is that whatever the hell he's doing, he's being blatantly obvious about it." Another pause. "They think it might be Robin Mills, sir."

"*Fuck.*" Robin Mills—the same kid who, three years

back, I'd brought up to my office in an attempt to intimidate out of professional gambling. It looked like he hadn't learned his lesson—time had only made him bolder.

I hopped out of bed and headed for my closet. I could have ordered Damien to get back to the casino security and tell them to kick him out or hold him until the police arrived and arrested him for trespassing, but after the day I'd had, an affront like that felt personal. I'd told the kid to his face to stay off The Palisade property, yet here he was. It was the last straw. His little stunt meant that he was going to receive the brunt of today's particularly awful brand of horrible.

It was time for me to let off a little steam.

"Apprehend him," I said while I shrugged on my shirt and did it up button by button. I wasn't going to waste time. "Tell security to take him to my office."

"To your office, sir?" Damien asked.

"That's what I said." I rolled up my cuffs, then pulled on my pants. "If it is Robin Mills, he's trespassing. He was banned from The Palisade three years ago. I won't stand by while he tries to suck me dry. If he puts up a fight, give security authorization to use force. Once he's secured, hold him in my office until I get there. I'm heading back in."

"I'll make sure the car is ready out front, and that security knows what steps to take," Damien said with a bow of his head. "Is there anything else I can do for you tonight, sir?"

I scoffed. "Do you want to give me some good news, Damien?"

There was silence for a moment, and I felt Damien study me, like he wasn't sure if I was being facetious or not. Then, finally, he cleared his throat. "I'm getting ready to propose to my boyfriend."

I hadn't been expecting him to reply with something serious, so I came to a stop, my hand on my undone belt buckle, my eyes on the bodyguard occupying the space beside the door. That explained the change in his mood over the last few months.

"Congratulations," I said, doing my best to sound sincere. While I was glad for him, I had my own struggles to overcome.

But if Damien could get over a personal loss and still find happiness, so could I—and it would start tonight, in my office, when I personally saw that burr in my side, Robin Mills, arrested for trespassing.

7

ROBIN

*A*nother purple chip hit the table. I pushed it forward with two fingers and was about to announce my intention to the dealer when a hand clamped down on my shoulder. It didn't come as a surprise. I'd been waiting for security to show up and do their job. If anything, it was disappointing that they'd taken this long.

"Sir," the security guard said softly into my ear. "I'm afraid you're too good for the game."

The classic line. I lifted a brow and leaned back in my chair until only the back feet remained on the ground. The guard pushed me back down, the chair landing with a sharp *clack!*

"What made you think that?" I asked with a grin, sliding my poker chip back across the table and lifting it between two fingers. I let it cascade down between my fingers, moving space to space, guided by my fingers, then brought it back up. It was something else to toy with five hundred dollars like it was nothing. Even now, years after having taken every casino in Nevada for everything they were worth, it boggled my mind how much money one little plastic disk could represent.

"I'll have to ask you to come with me," the guard said. It didn't look like he was going to answer my question. Even Troy's lax casino security knew better than to engage a troublemaker. At least he had that going for him.

With a sigh, I stood. My chips were still laid on the table, cashed into each of its boxes. Knowing I wouldn't be allowed much movement, I flipped the dealer the chip between my fingers.

"Thank you for an excellent game," I told her. She didn't touch the chip, nor did she move. Frozen in place, she kept her hands at her sides and fixed me with an easy, fabricated smile that told me she'd rather be anywhere but here. "The Barney is yours. I know they're going to confiscate the rest, but don't let them take that one from you. You earned it."

"Come along, sir," the security guard said. He set his hand on my shoulder again and pushed, forcing me to turn. "You've been asked to make an appearance elsewhere."

Oh, had I?

A hint of a grin lifted the corners of my lips, and I let myself be led away. Step one was complete, and, just like I'd planned, step two was well underway.

Troy, Troy, Troy.

Predictable as always.

I WAS TAKEN from the floor back to the lobby. The bouncers I'd passed on the way in were gone, likely being chewed out somewhere else for having let someone like me into the casino. Wherever they'd gone, I wished them well. It wasn't my intention to get anyone in trouble tonight.

At least, not anyone working the floor.

The security guard led me across the lobby to an elevator with a keypad. He input a string of numbers, then pressed the call button. The light behind the button blinked on and the elevator doors opened smoothly, revealing a large cabin with chrome walls.

"Step inside, please," the security guard said. I did as asked, and he followed behind me. Unlike in public use elevators, there were no floor number buttons. Another keypad had been wired into the cabin in their place. I watched the guard input a different string of numbers, then lost interest and looked at our reflections in the chrome doors as they closed. I didn't look anything other than average—a light blue button-down shirt, the top button undone, and black pants. My dark hair was a little messy from a long day of travel, but I was pleased to see that there were no bags under my eyes or other signs of fatigue evident on my face. My guard-escort was dressed in a suit, and would have been indistinguishable from any other of the well-dressed guests of the casino had it not been for the ID badge clipped to the right breast of his suit jacket.

According to his ID card, his name was S. *Killinger.* With a last name like that, it didn't surprise me the guy was working security.

"So." I folded my hands upon the small of my back and continued to watch our reflections in the door. "Killinger is a pretty cool name. Is it like, a pseudonym?"

No reply.

"What does the 'S' stand for? Steven? Skylar? Simon? You don't feel like a Simon to me. Steven really feels like it'd be a good fit."

Killinger's lips thinned. He didn't reply.

"I'm Robin," I said with a shrug, my grin starting to turn mischievous. "But, since you have me detained, you probably already know that."

Nothing.

"Come *on*." I let my head fall back and took a chance to get a look at the overhead paneling. Like in standard elevators, there was a service hatch. Unlike in most elevators, the ceiling was chrome-plated, too, and shined until it reflected. I took note of the security devices—or lack thereof—in the elevator before I sighed heavily and let my head drop forward again. "You were nice to me down in the pit. What changed? Did I offend you by following instructions instead of acting out? I bet you were expecting to have to cart me off, weren't you?"

No answer.

What a chatterbox Killinger was.

"Well... I'm sorry. I know you were—" The elevator came to a stop, and the doors parted. "Oh, we're here."

"Please follow me," Killinger said.

I did.

It had been three years since I'd last been in The Palisade's executive offices, and at the time, I'd been too outraged that I was being dragged up to corporate rather than discreetly shown the door and told to get lost to pay much attention to its layout. The elevator emptied into a long hallway stretching both left and right with doors on either side. The crystal glitz of the hotel and casino was gone—the place looked very much like any other boring corporate office. If I'd woken up here with no recollection of where I'd come from, I never would have guessed I was in a Vegas hotel.

Killinger brought me to the left and opened a door on the same side as the elevator. Inside was a room large enough to hold a ten-chair conference table with just enough room left over to walk around the perimeter. There were no windows and only one door. I remembered this place from my last time here—the dreaded holding room. They were going to try to bore me to death before bringing me out to slap my wrists.

Great.

I sank down into one of the office chairs and started to roll back and forth, chasing away the seconds. Killinger took up post in front of the door, his arms crossed over his chest, looking pissed as hell. I wasn't sure if it was my annoying line of questioning that had gotten beneath his skin, or if he really didn't want to be here.

Maybe it was a little of both. With a name like Killinger, and working security, he'd probably expected work to be a little more interesting. Babysitting a twenty-two-year-old card counter who wasn't looking to stir trouble wasn't exactly something to write home about.

Poor Killinger.

I wondered if I should cause some trouble just to make his life a little more entertaining. Soon enough, there'd be more than enough change around The Palisade to keep him on his toes, but until then, I felt like I owed him engagement. While Troy didn't handle his staff directly, he wasn't going out of his way to make their work more rewarding, either.

"What's the wildest thing you've ever done while working here?" I asked, coming to a stop to look Killinger's way. "If you've worked here for any length of time, I imagine you've seen some pretty weird stuff, and had to personally deal with most of it. I'm going to go out on a limb here and say that I'm not the kind of person you'd typically be dealing with during your shift."

Killinger's lips twitched with disdain. If he didn't stop, he was going to talk my ear off.

"Well," I sighed. "I guess that's fine. We can just sit here in this conference room and *not* talk. That's an option, too."

I waited a few seconds for a reply. When I received none, I wheeled back to the table and crossed my arms on it, then rested my head on top of them. If Killinger wasn't going to be chatty, then I'd go over what was about to happen and figure out how best to use it to my advantage. Steps one and two were underway, but with the third and final step yet to be achieved, my plan hadn't come to full fruition. There was always a chance something could go wrong.

And more than that, there was always a chance I was making a mistake.

It was a bold idea, and I was taking huge risks in order to see it through. There was every chance in the world that Troy wouldn't behave in a predictable manner, or that something would go wrong along the way, or that, when he found out who I was, he'd be more enraged than aroused, and have me arrested regardless. I was banking on my understanding of a man I'd only met once and maxing out a bet I couldn't afford to lose. If I was arrested, Monty would have to jump through hoops to make sure I got out again, and the last thing I wanted to do was cause him trouble.

But if my bet paid off?

Fuck, would it be worth it.

I set my worry aside and focused on the future. Out of three steps, two of them had already gone according to play. What did I have to worry about? I knew Troy—I'd looked into his head and gotten him all figured out. I *had* this.

By the end of the night, what was his would be *mine*.

I lifted my head from the table and opened my mouth, intending to ask Killinger another round of time-passing questions, when I heard a tinny voice speak quietly near the door. Someone was talking into Killinger's earpiece. Either there was trouble in the casino that the rest of the security team couldn't handle, or a certain Sullivan had arrived and was demanding to see me.

"We'll be there shortly," Killinger replied, one finger on his earpiece.

That answered that. It sounded like Troy had arrived and was ready to see me. There was no time for doubts—I'd made a decision, and I was going to stick to it. Troy's punishment for fucking up in such an astronomical way was simple: I was here now, and I'd make sure in the best way I could that he'd *never* fuck up again.

Master had come to play.

8

TROY

Three firm knocks on my office door echoed through the room. I lifted my chin and looked at the door, ready for what was to come. The kid I'd tried to scare off three years back had returned, made a fool of himself, and ruined the rest of his life. He'd chosen the wrong fucking night to come back, guns blazing, to my casino. I'd work my anger and frustration out on him, get him carted off, and then approach the rest of the day with the clear mind I needed in order to make the necessary changes to my business. I *would* make Master proud.

"Come in," I said, tone steely.

One of the solid wood doors opened. My head of security, Sam, pushed a familiar kid into the room. The kid, not so much a kid anymore, but a young man, stumbled, then found his footing and corrected his posture. He tugged at his sleeves and shot a look over his shoulder at Sam. "Really, Steven?"

Sam said nothing. He stood in the doorway, barricading the way out.

"You can go," I told Sam. "Shut the door behind you. I want to speak to Mr. Mills alone."

Sam bowed his head and made his exit. The door closed.

We were alone.

Robin brushed down the front of his shirt, lips curled in displeasure, and while he remained still, I took a moment to look him over. The years had changed him in subtle ways. The shape of his face remained the same, but the features on it had altered. His eyes, once young and bright, were more mature than I remembered, although they still gleamed with the same sharp intelligence and seething distaste as they had the last time we'd met. He'd kept the same haircut over the years—long, but pushed back from his face. Full, pink lips drew my eye, and I felt a twinge of guilt for even looking. What would Master think if he knew I'd noticed something like that about another man?

No matter what he thought, it wouldn't matter. When I

tore into Robin and had him escorted away by the police, Master would know that not only was I serious about changing the way I did business, but that I was serious about him. I would *not* disappoint him again.

"Three years ago, you were banned from The Palisade hotel and casino, and all properties belonging to it," I told Robin coolly, lacing my hands together on my desk. At full height, he was tall, and his slender frame was sleek. The look in his eyes made him seem foxlike, and their intense blue color did things to me that I preferred not to think about. I'd been single since I'd taken control of The Palisade over from my father, but submissive to Master for a little more than a year and a half. Some spunky, strapping delinquent wasn't going to steal me from him. Only Master could treat me like I needed to be treated and take the burden of my world off my shoulders. An arrogant young man like Robin Mills could never make me happy in the same way. "I'll give you one chance to explain yourself before I call the police."

Robin lifted a brow and shook his head. He ran a hand through his hair, shaking it out, then looked at me with a gaze ten times more intense than any I'd seen before. A jolt shot through my body, starting in my heart and ending in my groin. His arrogance was gone, and in its place emerged unshakable, mature confidence. The difference was subtle, but it was stunning. It was like Robin had gone from *thinking* he was better than me to *knowing* it. The look in his eyes told me that he owned me, and that standing in my office was nothing more than an amusing, if childish, excursion for him.

My cock twitched. Of all the ways this encounter could have gone, I hadn't been expecting it to go like this.

"You want me to explain myself?" The tone of his voice had darkened from when he'd first stumbled into the room and spoken to Sam. The sound of it sent another chilling jolt straight through me. My heart raced, and my pulse drummed in my ears. I *knew* that voice.

Robin stepped forward, a confident, playful sway to his hips. He kept his eyes locked on me. "Just one chance, Troy?"

I sat where I was, too stunned to say or do anything. My cock pushed against the front of my slacks, no longer willing to stay flaccid.

That voice.

Robin arrived at the other side of my desk, eyes holding my gaze, refusing to let me go. In my peripheral vision, I saw him reach into his back pocket and pull something out. It wasn't until I saw a flash of color that I understood what it was.

Red panties.

Pretty red lace panties, with ribbons done up over the front panel like a corset, where they'd tighten and hold his cock snug, outlining it.

My heart pounded against my rib cage, threatening to burst from my chest. Heat rose up my neck and washed over my face.

"I don't think I'm the one who needs to explain himself," Robin—*Master*—told me. He dropped his panties on my desk, his eyes never leaving mine. "I'm not the only one who's been bad. Now, why don't you tell me... what are you planning to do about it?"

9

TROY

"*M*aster?" The breath caught in my throat. I knew I was gawking, but how could I do anything but? Robin Mills, the kid who'd lifted tens of thousands of dollars from my casino while under-age, was the one I called Master, the one I'd given an allowance to, let into my accounts, and showered gifts onto for the drug I needed—the all-powerful "no."

I'd never seen his picture, and while a time or two I'd caught his blurred reflection off a surface in the pictures he'd sent while spending my money, I'd never pieced together that it could be him. But all this time, he'd known it was me. My identity had never been a secret.

He'd come to the casino tonight and made brazen displays not because he was a dumb kid who hadn't learned his lesson, but because he knew, after the day I'd had, that I'd make an example out of him. He'd wanted me to take him up to my office and get him alone, and I'd played into his plan perfectly.

Master was here to punish me.

"Very good, Troy." Master set a hand on my desk and leaned forward, his slender fingers wrapping around my tie. He continued to hold my gaze, refusing to let me go. The blue of his irises burned through me, so fierce that, despite our size difference, I felt like I was the one at a disadvantage. "Now, will you tell me who's the one in trouble?"

Arousal rolled through me, leaving me helpless against his word. Weak, I replied, "Me, Master. I'm the one in trouble."

"Yes, you are. Good boy." He tugged gently on my tie, effortlessly drawing me toward him. I was too stunned to do anything but obey. Without even knowing that Robin was Master, my body had responded to him. His command over me was so deeply ingrained that my body had submitted to him before my mind had pieced together who he was.

Master tugged my tie upward, a suggestion rather than a

demand. I rose to my feet, following it, not wanting to disappoint him. I was broader and several inches taller than he was—tall enough that he had to tilt his head to look into my eyes when I was at my full height—but there was no mistaking our dynamic. Master was the one in charge, and he had been since the first day of our arrangement. The fact that he was Robin Mills didn't factor into how I felt. I was loyal, and I was devoted. The past was forgotten. All that mattered was the future.

"Do you remember what I said earlier today?" Master asked. He lifted an eyebrow expectantly when he spoke, almost breaking me. He was more gorgeous in person than I could have imagined. "What I said when we were texting?"

For a terrifying moment, my mind went blank. My thoughts tripped over themselves, struggling to get over the look in Master's eyes and the way having him here in person made me feel. What had he said? He'd been disappointed. And...

The memory struck me in the chest and left me breathless.

"You told me that I would be punished," I said hoarsely. "And that... you'd teach me how to look after myself."

Master afforded me a smirk. Slowly, he wrapped my tie around his hand, forcing me to hunch over until we were nose to nose. This close, I could smell subtle notes of omega beneath the woodsy scent of his aftershave. How decadent it was that an omega could control me this way —that someone so much smaller and younger than me could own me body and soul. It made every "no" so much better, and every punishment that much more arousing. "I did, didn't I?"

I noticed when his lips moved to speak, and when they quirked to the side in amusement. I'd never wanted to kiss someone so badly, but I knew better than to touch without permission. It didn't matter that sparks were going off like fireworks in my chest, or that my mind was choked with want for him—until he granted me permission, I wasn't allowed to touch.

"I guess I should tell you what's going to happen now that I'm here," Master said casually. "Are you ready to accept the biggest punishment you've ever received, Troy?"

A shiver shot down my spine, and I spoke before I knew I was doing it. "*Yes.*"

My eagerness pleased Master. He grinned, then tilted his head to the side and brushed the tip of his nose along mine. My knees gave out, and I had to grasp the edge of my desk to keep from stumbling. Arousal pulsed in my veins to the same rhythm as my heart, turning my blood red-hot.

"Good boy," Master whispered. I felt his words against my lips. "Drop to your knees. You're going to welcome your new boss the best way you can—with that pretty little mouth of yours."

I DROPPED to my knees without a second thought, not caring how Master's hold on my tie made it tighten around my neck. I deserved the discomfort for being bad. And now, given instructions, I'd show Master that I could be *good*.

Master dropped my tie, then reached down and tugged the knot loose so it was no longer snug against my neck. He run a hand through my hair, pushing it back from my face, then lifted his brow again in an expression I was quickly coming to adore. "Aren't you eager?"

I held my tongue. Right now, I couldn't afford to mess things up. Master had come a long way to punish me, and done incredible things in order to see me in person. I would be good for him. I would show him that I was his.

"If I didn't know better, I'd say you wanted this." He hummed, then looked away from me and tugged open his belt. When it sagged, he undid his fly and lowered the zipper beneath, tempting me with a partial view of the plain boxer-briefs he wore. His stiffened cock pushed against them, its outline distinct. I imagined how fantastic it would look behind red lace and ribbons. "Do you want this, Troy? Tell me."

"I do, Master," I told him. My cock ached for touch and my body longed for release, but Master came first. I would use my mouth to welcome him into my world, and I would do it for however long he wanted. "Please, let me welcome you. I'm ready."

Master tilted his head to the side. Then, smirk ever-present on his face, he slid his thumbs beneath the elastic of his boxer-briefs and lowered them. The shaft hidden behind the fabric came into view, long and thick enough to be satisfying without being too much. With it exposed, he left his boxer-briefs around his thighs and ran a hand through my hair, then pushed my head forward. "Suck."

I didn't need to be told again. I took him into my mouth, savoring his smooth tip before taking his length as deeply as I could. He shivered with pleasure for me, so I kept taking him in, sucking and lapping like I'd been born to do it.

"Oh, *fuck*," Master whispered under his breath. He tightened his fingers in my hair, guiding me back and forth on his dick. I followed obediently. "That's right, Troy. Fucking *suck* me. You like it, don't you? You like having me down your throat..."

He pushed forward suddenly, holding my head in place. Tears beaded in the corners of my eyes, but I hummed contently to let Master know that what he said was right. I was *his*, and whatever he wanted me to do, I would do.

"If you keep your lips tight like that, I'm going to come down your throat," Master warned me. In response, I tightened my lips, and he moaned. While there'd been times in the past where my conversations with Master had turned sexual, nothing had ever been like this. To be able to see the pleasure touching him brought fulfilled me. At last, I was able to give back in a meaningful way to the man who'd given me purpose and helped me aspire to greatness. It flooded my chest with warmth.

"You naughty little thing," Master whispered. He was moving his hips now, pistoning into my mouth as I held my lips taut. "You want me to come inside you, don't you? You want to suck all my cum down."

I hummed affirmatively, and my cock throbbed. I wanted to taste him.

Master shivered. It ran through his whole body, into his thighs, and brought him to thrust into me a few times in rapid succession. The hand securing the back of my head held me in place, helping him push the deepest he'd been yet. Tears streamed down my cheeks, but I allowed him as far as he wanted to go and did my best to hold my lips tight for him. I wanted him to come more than I wanted it for myself.

"Oh, fuck. Here it comes. Are you ready for me, Troy?" He was breathless in a way I'd never heard before, and it excited me. Pleasure tingled in my groin, and I found myself pushing forward with my hips, humping the air as Master fucked my face. "Swallow it. Swallow it all. If you let a drop of it escape, you'll lick it off the floor until I say it's clean."

Yes. *Yes.*

Fireworks went off in my head. I gave my body over completely to Master, and as I did, his balls clenched, and he emptied into me. I moaned and swallowed it as instructed, not letting a single drop fall. When I was done, I lapped his dick clean.

He looked down at me, eyes still lidded with lust. "What a good boy you've been, Troy."

I rested my head on his thigh and caught my breath. The taste of him was on my tongue, and I committed it to memory. After so long spent talking on the phone and through text, he was *here*.

Master took a small step back and pushed my head so that I was looking up at him. When we'd reestablished eye contact, he spoke again. "But good isn't going to save you. What happened? It was terrible, but it was also completely avoidable. How long have I been after you to be more attentive? All the times you've botched the figures, all the little details you've let slip you by... if you'd listened, you could have prevented some of your loss."

It was true. I wanted to lower my head and close my eyes, but Master held me in place.

"So, your punishment is as follows." Master's hand left my head and wove around my tie instead. Slowly, he guided me to my feet. "Before, your money was my money, and everything you earned, you earned for me." Master's gaze was on me again, his eyes burning right through me. "But now? Everything about you belongs to me. Your money, your business, and your body."

I was achingly hard already, and hearing him take possession of me so fully almost pushed me over the edge. My balls clenched, and I had to hold back from coming.

Master smirked at me, playful and impossibly sexy. His eyes shone, and in that moment, I felt like a prized and coveted possession—something of value to him, and something that would continue to produce value as the days, weeks, and months went on. It made me want to try my hardest to *always* make him look at me like that. I could give him all the money in the world, but it would never have the same effect.

The look remained as Master finished what he had to say. "You're mine now, Troy. You might own The Palisade, but now, I own *you,* and you report to me. Is that an agreeable arrangement?"

It was an easy answer—I would give him anything he wanted. "Yes, Master."

"Then let's put our agreement to the test." Master nodded at my office chair, but his eyes remained locked on me. "Take your pants off, Troy, and sit down. I want to play with what's mine."

10

ROBIN

*T*roy sank into his office chair, the leather groaning beneath his sudden weight. In his hurry to obey, he'd neglected to take off his slacks. Realizing it, he scrambled to undo his belt and fly, then shoved his pants down his thighs. A proud, thick cock sprang out from beneath his boxers, its tip already glistening. I'd already come, but seeing it made me want to ride it in the worst way.

Was it irresponsible of me? Yes. I knew it even as I stepped out of my shoes and pushed my pants and boxer-briefs the rest of the way down. But more than anything, I wanted to own the man who'd treated me so poorly when I was at my worst. I wanted him to understand that the kid he'd treated with such unkindness was now the one who called the shots.

"Where is your lube, Troy?" I demanded. I knew that he kept some in his office—there'd been more than one time I'd ordered him to insert a plug into himself while on the job.

He pointed at one of his desk drawers. "In there."

I didn't ask for permission. What was his was now mine, and I'd partake of it freely. I pulled open the drawer, took the bottle of lube from inside, and squirted some into the palm of my hand. Then I unceremoniously fisted his cock and stroked it over his shaft and head, making sure to get beneath his ridge.

Troy shivered and moved his hips, pumping subtly into my hand. His body was wound tight with excitement, and I figured that it wouldn't be long after I started to ride that he'd come.

With that in mind, I set the bottle aside and straddled his lap, slipping my legs beneath the armrests so we were chest to chest. His wet cock brushed up between my cheeks, making him moan in anticipation. "When I told you that you belong to me entirely, I meant it," I told him. "The cum in your balls and your orgasm belong to me, too.

If you come before I say you can, you *will* be punished. You're not going to like what happens to you when I'm here to punish you in person, Troy. I promise you that."

He made a warbling, affirmative sound in his throat that made me grin. At forty-six years old, Troy had decades on me. He was more powerful and more successful. Descended from a long line of businessmen, he'd been raised to do great things, yet here he was, submissive to me.

I lifted my hips and wiggled my ass, then reached around and held his cock upright. Slowly, making sure he felt it, I lowered myself onto it. No matter how I tried to open myself for him, he stretched me. It had been years since I'd been with a man, and although I'd had toys to keep me company, there was no comparing them to Troy.

I took in a shuddering breath and pushed down onto him, taking him deeper. All the while, thoughts ran through my head, encouraging me to keep going. *Mine. All mine. Need to show him who he belongs to. Need to show him that he's my new toy.*

Pleasure like this was selfish, but it was what I needed. As he stretched me, I pushed harder, then rolled my hips and established a rhythm that had him pushing against my prostate in perfect time. Pleasure bloomed low in my gut, and I let it push me onward.

More. More. *More.*

"Pump my cock," I ordered Troy, sounding every bit as breathless as I felt. I'd gotten hard again, and I knew I had a second orgasm in me. I held onto the top of his office chair and moved with greater urgency, bringing myself closer to coming with every new rock of my hips. "I wanna come all over you. Wanna... wanna get it all over your shirt."

Troy's pupils were blown out with lust, and his eyes were partially lidded from pleasure. Enslaved by my words, he took hold of my cock and started to pump. The touch of his hand sent pinpricks of pleasure through me, and I thrust into the tightness of his palm greedily with each upward motion.

"Master, please." His voice was thin and fearful—he knew that speaking without my permission would get him punished. "I'm going to... I can't..."

"Don't come." I squeezed the top of the chair, clenching my teeth against the sudden peak of pleasure that swept through me. "Don't you dare come yet."

"*Master.*" His voice was thin and pleading, and it almost

broke me. It was small, weak, and uncertain, and it showed me how deeply Troy's submissive streak ran. He didn't want to go against my word, but his body was going to betray him, and he was turning to me for help. *Me.* "Master, *please...*"

Impulse rose inside me, and before I knew what I was doing, I was kissing him. Our lips crushed together as I bounced on his cock, and I kissed him like I needed him, too turned on from hearing his true submission to not acknowledge it in some way.

"Come," I whispered against his lips. "Come, Troy."

I pressed my forehead to his and sank down, letting him thrust into me deep. In seconds, I felt his thick cock throbbing for me, emptying its seed into my body.

Mine. All mine.

With a quivering cry, I came as well, striping his shirt with what was left in my balls. I hadn't intended to stay on his lap after the deed was done, but I found myself resting my head on his broad shoulder regardless, then closing my eyes as the aftermath of orgasm hit. His softening cock remained lodged in my ass, and I found myself liking how it felt, like our bodies had been made to fit together just like this.

How strange it was that the man I'd hated could bring me pleasure like no one else. Even if this turned out to be a horrible idea and nothing ended up changing, this moment alone was worth it. Troy was really something else. Arrogant, and self-centered, and pigheaded, but...

I smiled.

For now, he was mine.

11

ROBIN

It was four in the morning by the time I made it back to my condo, but even though I was exhausted, I was too wired to sleep. Before I could do anything else, I needed to turn my mind off, and that meant familiarizing myself with my surroundings and getting comfortable.

I'd seen pictures of the condo online—Monty had bought it for me after Rent-a-Dom took off in its second year, because he'd known that one day, I'd be coming back. When we'd been young and impulsive, it had been our goal to take Vegas by storm, and for the most part, it had worked. It'd just taken a little while to get there.

I found the kitchen and checked the fridge. A small container of coffee creamer had been left in the door, which told me that there was coffee waiting for me some-where. It would wait until tomorrow, when I'd need it to stay awake. For now, I needed a snack that would stop my growling stomach so I could focus on passing out for the night.

"What did you get me, Monty..." I mumbled under my breath as I poked around in the fridge. All the basics were there—milk, eggs, a carton of orange juice... and a serving-sized resealable container. I narrowed my eyes and picked it up, looking at what was inside through the transparent plastic. Beige, liquidy...

Overnight oats.

I rolled my eyes.

Apparently, Monty wanted to make sure I had a hearty, bowel-happy breakfast waiting for me on my first morning back in town. Or maybe he'd mistaken me for a horse. Either way, overnight oats would do just fine. It was almost a decent hour in the morning, anyway. I figured they'd had plenty of time to sit.

I searched the kitchen drawers until I found a spoon, then went to sit on the couch in the living room. As I settled, I took my phone from my pocket and shot Monty a text.

Arrived safe and sound at the condo. Thank you for

making sure there was food waiting for me, and for the overnight oats. You make me feel like an old man.

I pulled the top off the oats and poked at them with my spoon. As I started to mix them, I noticed something out of the ordinary—a swirl of color. I knew what it was right away and grinned. Responsible people sweetened their oats with honey or brown sugar, but Monty knew me better than that. He'd picked up the same sugar dino eggs we'd gone crazy for as kids and hidden them in the oatmeal to turn bland, old-fashioned oats not so boring anymore.

I grinned like a total dork and stirred again, swirling the coloring, then sent another text to Monty. *Scratch the old man part. I can't believe you put dino eggs in my oats. SO COOL. I've got the biggest, goofiest grin on my face right now. Omg, you have no idea how much I needed this.*

My phone buzzed with a response. *You might not feel like an old man, but you make me feel like a nervous parent. Christian said that you had other business to attend to tonight? What were you up to? Is everything okay?*

Christian, huh? That must have been the driver's name. I snorted. *Yeah, everything's fine. I just came into possession of a casino, is all.*

Robin.

The one-word reply made me laugh harder than it should have, and I almost sent my overnight oats flying. To make sure I didn't spill anything, I set them down on the table by the couch and stretched out like a cat, stretching both my legs out as far as they could go before flopping into a comfortable position. *What? You told me to take some time for myself.*

I didn't mean it like that, and you know it.

That was true. I set my phone on my chest and reached for my oats, eating a few spoonfuls before I resumed the conversation. *If you thought I was going to come to Vegas and bum around for the next few months, you've clearly forgotten that I'm a Mills, too. When it comes to keeping busy, we don't really have an off button.*

There was a pause. I used it to eat the rest of my oats, then set the container aside.

Besides, I typed, *what are you doing up at four in the morning? Don't you have a business you should be running? ;)*

Blame the Mills genes on that one, Monty replied. *I got home from a Toby's Troubles concert at around one this morning and couldn't get to sleep. I figured I'd use the time to get some work done. Businesses run just as well at four in the morning as they do during daylight hours.*

And I'm the one who should be taking care of himself? I yawned. Vegas' four in the morning was Rockport's seven in the morning, and after a full day of travel and corporate takeover, I was starting to feel it. *It'll be fine. Don't worry about it, okay? I've got it under control.*

I hope you do, Monty replied. *I could swoop in and save you from a bad RaD contract, but casino management? That's not something I can wave my magic wand and fix.*

I wouldn't want you to, I answered. *I've got this in the bag, Monty. How many casinos have I gutted during my career? I know the industry from the most important perspective—the one trying to profit from and exploit it. It's going to be cake.*

I glanced in the direction of the kitchen. Cake sounded good right about now.

Monty's reply was delayed, which meant that he wasn't necessarily on board with what I had to say. *You know best. Just... be careful, Robin. There's a difference between being a digital Dom and living the lifestyle day in and day out with a submissive you can touch. I'm not trying to warn you off from doing it, but I need you to make sure you know what you're getting into.*

I buzzed my lips. Monty was worried over nothing. What I had with Troy wasn't like that. *I'll be careful. Promise. I need to get to sleep now, though. I've got to be up in a few hours, and it's going to be a hell of a busy day.*

Sleep well.

Night.

Monty didn't text me again after that, so I set my phone aside and closed my eyes. The couch was comfortable, and after so long spent on my feet doing things, I found I didn't want to move again. It was probably better here, anyway. In bed, there'd be space for me to toss and turn, remembering the way Troy had felt beneath me, and how his touch had sent pinpricks of pleasure down my spine.

12

TROY

The second I stepped out of the elevator and onto the executive floor, I knew something was wrong. Westward loitered in the hallway nearby, his shoulders hunched as he wrung his hands nervously. Sweat beaded his brow, and he mumbled something under his breath, like he was rehearsing what he was going to tell me right up to the last minute. As it was, he looked a minute or two away from a nervous breakdown. I was glad that I hadn't had my driver stop to get a coffee this morning—if I'd been any later, he might have made so much friction between his palms that he'd spontaneously combust.

"Good morning, Westward," I said with as much heart as I

could. "You look... *stressed* this morning. What's going on?"

"Sir!" Westward snapped to attention. He flung his hands apart, then thought better of it and started to wring them all over again. Any second now, I was sure his fingers were going to catch fire. "Thank goodness you're here, sir. There's... there's been an *incident*."

The words left a bitter taste in my mouth. "The last time you said there was an incident, I ended up losing millions of dollars. What's going on this time? Do we need to have a private talk in my office?"

"That's the thing, sir," Westward said desperately. He looked down the hall at the door leading to my office, then sighed and shook his head. "Lena called me in a panic this morning, sir."

"Lena?" What did my secretary have to be worried about?

Westward nodded emphatically. "Yes, sir. Lena. She... she says that there's someone in your office, sir. She's tried to make him leave, but he refuses to move. He's in your *chair*, sir. At your desk. She even tried to squirt him with a squirt bottle of water, sir, like she says she uses on her cats when they're clawing the curtains... but he found one of your plastic paper protectors and he's become quite adept at using it like a shield."

I knew that for Westward and Lena, the situation was serious, but I couldn't help but bust out laughing. "You're using a spray bottle on him?"

"He won't move!" Westward's face had turned red. If he got any brighter, I'd be able to hang him from a Christmas tree like an ornament. "We threatened to call security on him, but he told us that if we did, you'd be upset. He had your personal phone number, sir! What was I supposed to do? I don't know how he got up here, or got into your office, or got your number, but it's *not right*."

I sucked my stomach in and held back another round of laughter. I didn't need to see who was at my desk to know who it was—it looked like Master had been sincere about what he'd said the day before. He was going to step in and take charge. While I had no idea if he knew what he was doing in terms of business decisions, I knew that having him there would help me pull myself back together. Yesterday, I'd felt like I was facing an insurmountable obstacle following Redding's betrayal and the restructuring it necessitated, but with Master there to supervise me, everything would be okay. With him around, I could see through my panic. It didn't matter how large the obstacles in my way were—I'd find a way around them just so I could see him smile again.

With him here, I'd find a way.

"Mr. Sullivan, sir!" Westward said impatiently. "I don't know what's gotten into you this morning. If you need to take a day to yourself after what happened yesterday, then please do so, but first, please authorize me to send in security and have him removed!"

"There's no need, Westward." I chuckled, then shook my head. "Mr. Mills is stepping in to act as my assistant while we work through the fallout from the Redding catastrophe. He'll be here regularly, and is to be granted free access to my office."

Westward squinted at me, his eyes so narrow, they looked like they were closed. "A-A-Assistant?"

"It happened late in the day yesterday, long after you'd gone home for the day." I offered Westward an apologetic smile. "I should have notified you and Lena both, but it slipped my mind. There were a few other pressing things I was dealing with."

Like Master's ass on my lap, my cock lodged deep inside of him. The way he'd rocked and moaned on top of me, unashamed to take exactly what he wanted...

I bit down on my lip and snapped out of my daydreams. If Westward saw me getting hard, I was pretty sure he'd melt down.

"You haven't even seen who it is, sir," Westward argued. "He looks very young. Wouldn't you be better off with a senior assistant? Someone who's had more experience in the industry?"

"I'll consider it." I was in too good a mood to let Westward's skepticism get me down. "Thank you for taking care of a potentially troublesome issue. When I see Lena on my way in, I'll let her know that Mr. Mills is to be give admission into my office at will."

"Well... okay, sir." Westward sighed. "Please apologize to *Mr. Mills* for the squirt bottle incident. We were panicked and didn't know what else to do."

"You're a good man, Westward. Thank you. I'll look into getting squirt guns for the next time someone infiltrates the executive offices." I clapped him on the shoulder while he gaped at me, then headed down the hall to the door that let into the small reception area Lena worked in. My office was accessible through it.

I opened the door to find her standing in the doorway to my office, both doors flung open, dual squirt bottles in hand. Her dark hair was twisted up in a tight bun, and she was in her stocking feet, her heels left haphazardly by her desk. The tight pencil skirt she'd worn in this morning was rolled up to scandalous levels to give her more mobility, and she used it to broaden her stance and take up as much of the doorway as she could.

When I entered, she looked over her shoulder, war in her eyes. The expression faded when she noticed it was me.

"Mr. Sullivan!" Lena squeaked. She hurriedly put one of the squirt bottles down and rolled down her skirt, but kept the other bottle in hand, ready for combat. I noticed that there was a rubber band stuck to the side of her head, caught in her hair. "I'm so glad you're here. There is a *delinquent* in your office."

"Westward told me," I said with a nod.

"I've been trying to get him to leave, but he won't move. He's taken up station on your office chair. I wanted to call security, but he has—" She lowered her voice, "—*personally revealing information* about you, and he's using it like a weapon."

"My phone number?" I asked as flatly as I could, trying to hold back laughter.

"I don't know how he got it, sir!" Lena insisted. "I never

give out your personal number. If someone asks, I say that it's not on file, and that you keep your life very private. Wherever he got it, it wasn't from me!"

"It's fine," I said.

Lena furrowed her brow. "Fine? Did you get a new phone number?"

"No." I finally gave in and laughed. "The young man in my office is Mr. Mills, and he'll be here helping me while we navigate the situation with Redding."

Much like Westward, Lena squinted at me. She opened her mouth and was about to speak when a sound like a guitar string being plucked interrupted us. A rubber band shot through the doorway and landed on the floor a few feet from her, having narrowly missed her shoulder. In a rage, Lena spun around and fired into my office with her squirt bottle. She held it with both hands like she was handling a gun. I heard, but didn't see, water splatter against plastic.

When I did bring those squirt guns into the office, she was going to dominate the competition.

"Stand down, Lena," I said with a chuckle. I came to stand at her side and set a hand on her shoulder. From there, I saw Master seated at my desk. His dark brown hair was combed back, and he was dressed in a finely fitted suit. The blue tie he wore brought out the color of his eyes, and I found myself having to make an effort not to lose myself to them. "Why don't you go put your shoes back on and get back to business as usual? Mr. Mills won't open fire on you anymore."

Lena eyed my master suspiciously, then slowly shook her head and looked up at me. I took the chance to pluck the rubber band from her hair. "He's a menace, that one."

"I'm sure once he's not being squirted at, he'll fit in just fine."

Lena's eyes sharpened. "I hope you're right."

I hoped so, too.

By the time I got Lena settled back at her desk and made my way into the office, Master had put the protective plastic sheet aside. Papers were spread out across the desk, luckily undamaged by the squirt bottle incident. I recognized what they were instantly—reports from the last several years of board meetings, and structural documents containing our latest business practices and staffing goals. Master pored over them. When I closed the door, he looked up at me, unimpressed. "Really, Troy?"

I hesitated, unsure if I should speak, or if I should keep my silence. I decided to play it safe and wait to see what he had to say.

Master gestured at the paperwork in front of him. "Is this really how you run your business?"

I wanted to speak, but knew better. Instead, I stood near the door and waited for instruction. While I knew Master was smart and ambitious, running a business required certain skills and understanding I wasn't sure he possessed. With time and practice, he'd be a pro, but as an uneducated outsider, he probably had very little clue what he was looking at. When he'd told me he'd teach me how to take care of myself, I'd assumed he meant emotionally, not professionally. How was I supposed to politely inform him that he had no clue what he was talking about?

"I knew that you were stubborn, but I didn't realize it went this far." Master sighed. He leaned back in my chair and twisted it from side to side. "This business model reads like it's from the 1950s. We're going to need to restructure completely. I think some parts can be salvaged, but the rest is going to need to go. If you want to succeed in a constantly evolving world, you're going to have to get with the times and be willing to embrace change as it comes."

I hesitated, surprised by the ease with which he spoke. For the last year and a half of our relationship, our conversations had been focused either on me, or on the things that Master had bought with my money. Who was he, behind the mask he wore? I realized that I only knew Master, not Robin Mills.

What was his story?

There was more to him than card counting and domination. What was he capable of?

"Mm, this is going to get complicated if you can't talk." Master crossed his arms on the edge of the desk, careful not to disturb the paperwork upon it. "While we're in the office, you can speak freely, Troy. And, for discretion's sake, you can call me Mr. Mills or Robin. We're not going to be able to get to work if you're constantly in your submissive state, are we?"

"No," I agreed. I stepped forward, my gaze set on him. There was a strange rift inside me, tearing me apart. It was hard to think of him as anything but Master, but here, things were different. I had to figure out a way to get over the shift.

"Good," he said. "Then since we're in agreement," he gestured at the paperwork again, "I got here early this morning to go over all the documents I could find. I know that this isn't everything, but what I *was* able to find gave me a pretty comprehensive look at how The Palisade is run at an executive level, especially when it comes to profits. Tell me... have you changed things at all since you took over from dear old dad? Because everything I've come across reeks of clinging to old practices, even when it means loss of profits."

"Loss of profits?" I bristled. While I had a great deal of respect for Master, he was being unfair. I knew what I was doing. I'd been raised a Sullivan, and I'd learned what was best for our business. Running a hotel and casino wasn't like running any other kind of business in the world. It required insider knowledge, advanced mathematics, understanding of—

"Yes, loss of profits." Master narrowed his eyes. "Your focus is on bringing business into the casino right now, and while that wouldn't be such a bad thing if you adjusted your house advantages correctly and updated your machines—we'll get to that in a second—have you not been following outside business reports?"

The more he spoke, the less certain I became of myself. I'd thought that Master was an outsider to the industry, but he spoke with such confidence that I was beginning to feel like he wasn't making it up. Who was he?

"I... well, no."

Master covered his eyes with his hand. "Troy."

"The Palisade earned over a billion dollars last year," I defended. "The casino industry in Vegas generated almost twenty-five billion dollars in revenue. I think we're right to focus on casino-earned revenue."

Master parted his fingers in a V to look at me. "And that's down almost a billion dollars from the year before. Every year, casino earnings have been plummeting. Gaming is lagging, Troy. If you'd followed the reports and studied the current trends, you'd have seen that. More money is being spent on restaurants and entertainment, while gambling is down. You're not wrong to want to keep your casino healthy, but if you focused on other parts of your business—particularly your hotel and the restaurant in it— you'd be seeing a drastic surge in profits."

All I could do was stand there, stunned. Master knew

figures off the top of his head that I didn't expect anyone to know.

"You look like I just slapped you across the face with a giant fish," Master mused. "I know what I'm talking about, you know. I wouldn't be here sitting in your executive office acting like I owned the place if I had no idea how to take care of it. I like my belongings more than that—I'd have enough humility to hire someone who knows what the hell they're talking about if I didn't have a clue what was going on."

"Right." I hesitated, astounded. At twenty-two years old, Master was barely eligible for an undergraduate degree. To an extent, business could be taught, just like my father had taught me, but if Master was so successful, what was he doing counting cards and working for Rent-a-Dom? There was a piece of the puzzle I was missing, and it bothered me.

"So." Master sat back heavily. "All things considered, I'm going to need to see the most recent reports so I can get a handle on what's really going on, and what needs to be done. That being said, I've already put together a rudimentary plan of action. When you've got time, we'll sit down and discuss it. I've come up with suggestions on how to improve this quarter's profits, how to restructure staff roles and staff benefits from the floor all the way to the ceiling, and what policies and practices will need to be changed in order to turn The Palisade from a decent casino on the Strip into *the* casino on the Strip."

As I listened to him speak, it struck me all at once what was different about him. Master spoke in seductive, dark, and brooding tones, but the man who sat at my desk wasn't him. Master was gone, and Robin had taken his place. When he wasn't in his Dom headspace, he was quirky, snarky, and sharply intelligent. The contrast was stunning. For the first time, I was getting to know Master as a person instead of as a sexual object, and I found myself wanting to know more.

"Where did you learn all this?" I asked, mystified.

"Oh." Robin laughed. "Family stuff. You know how it is. You go in with your brother on your own company, life comes and drops a nuclear bomb in your lap, you take off and do what you need to do while he stays behind to hold down the fort... basic stuff."

I stared at him.

Robin rolled his eyes. "In other words, I have indirect business experience through helping my brother and listening to his troubles. I have insider knowledge about

Vegas and casinos because—as you're well aware—I used to be a professional gambler."

"You used to count cards," I said flatly. "There's a difference."

"And this is exactly why you need me." He smirked. It was so full of mischief and life that it made me smirk, too. "You're the stuffy suit from a long line of stuffy suits, and your perspective is narrowed to what's happening on the inside of your business. Me? Not so much. I'm going to call it like it is, whether you like it or not."

"I know you will. You've never been afraid to do it before."

"And you know why that is?" He lifted a brow and didn't wait for me to reply. "Because you can do better. You can do *so* much better. And, frankly, I don't care if what I say hurts your feelings if it ends up helping you in the long run. I'm not going to stand by and let you drive your business into the ground when you should be soaring—that's not how I operate."

My heart clenched. No one had ever treated me that way before. Robin didn't care that I was successful already like so many other people did. What he saw in me was potential, and he wanted to help me reach it. Support like that meant more to me than any pat on the back or words of praise.

If Robin wanted more, I would give it to him.

"So, when do we begin?" Robin asked.

I smiled. That was an easy one. "Right now."

13

ROBIN

I set Troy up with a small desk to the side of the room, near his filing cabinets, where he could work without interrupting me. At first, I'd been nervous that he wouldn't respect my authority in person and dismiss me because of my age, but Troy impressed me with his devotion to submission. Even when he was uncertain about how well I'd manage to run his business, he'd been willing to listen to what I had to say. That was a lot more than I could say about some of the other men I'd encountered during my time touring casino to casino. I liked that about him.

The day was spent partially in discussion about my plans for The Palisade's future, and partly working quietly on refining those plans on my own. Troy had standard business to attend to, so I let him work while I took care of my work. By the time five o'clock rolled around, I had the headache to end all headaches and an empty stomach that had started to grate on my nerves. Troy and I had been so caught up in my work that I'd forgotten to take lunch. Being hangry was a real thing, and I was total proof of it.

I clicked the top of the pen in my hand to draw back the nib, then closed Troy's laptop and wheeled back from his desk. If I didn't get something in me soon, I was going to have to snack on Westward.

"Are you done for the day?" Troy asked. He'd turned around from his desk, one arm looped over the back of his chair. I didn't like to admit it, but in that spread pose, with his suit on and his hair mussed from worrying, he was handsome.

"Yeah." I yawned and stood. "I didn't get very much sleep last night—for whatever reason—" I raised a brow suggestively, "and I came in early this morning to put together a plan, so I'm exhausted. I'm going to head out and report back in tomorrow. I've got the revisions to my plan almost sorted, so I figure I'll wrap it up tomorrow and we can go over them again before starting to roll out early implementation."

What was I going to eat for dinner tonight? Something

greasy was singing my name. Screw Monty and his oats—I was going for a burger. Fries sounded good, too. And a milkshake...

"What are you up to tonight?" Troy asked, pulling me from my food fantasies.

"Oh." I hesitated. I *liked* Troy, even if he was a stubborn dunderhead, but I hadn't come to The Palisade expecting to be overly social with him. Our text-based relationship happened on an irregular basis several times a week, and after last night's session, I hadn't thought he'd want to go again. "I'm going to find something to eat, then sleep for the next five years. I'm on East Coast time right now."

Troy smiled in a sincere, meaningful kind of way that got right under my skin and made me shiver. He looked *kind* when he did that, not like the unprofessional tyrant who'd personally kicked me out of his casino, and whose life I now controlled. "Let me take you out somewhere."

"I'm just going to head home." I shrugged. A little white lie wouldn't hurt. "I don't really... you know."

Do that.

Going out to dinner with Troy felt way too much like a date, and with the way his smile got to me, I didn't want to risk it. I was Troy's Dom, not his boyfriend. If he wanted to find someone to invite for dinner, he could go down to the casino and find any young man with stars in his eyes. That definitely wasn't me.

"Oh." Troy blinked, then clued in. "*Oh.*"

He got up from his chair and turned to face me in full, giving me his total attention.

"I didn't mean as a date," Troy admitted sheepishly. His tone of voice suggested the opposite. "It's your first day in the office, and the proposal you've pitched is fantastic. It'd be as business associates... that's all."

Business associates. That was cute. Despite being hangry, I found it charming that Troy would go to such lengths just to take me out for something to eat. Besides, we could keep talking about business. It was a Mills move to go on vacation and end up living and breathing work, but I was excited by the prospect of proving myself, just like my brother had.

And at the end of the day, whether I ate alone or with company, Troy was footing the bill, anyway.

"If that's the case, sure." I pulled at my tie, loosening its knot a little. "But, here are the rules: you will not order for me or speak on my behalf to restaurant staff, I will not pretend to be your boyfriend if an old flame shows up just so you can look macho, and you need to take me some-place I can get a burger." I paused. "And maybe a shake."

Troy laughed. "Done."

I hesitated. "You... don't want to take me out for fancy steak or escargot or sushi served off some poor, misguided, naked girl?"

"Oh." Troy's face fell. "So you probably don't want to go to the burger place I was thinking of, then. They serve the burgers deconstructed on former underwear models—male or female, your pick—and the fries come on the side, served in the cups of padded bras."

I stared at him.

Troy's lips trembled, then he burst out laughing. "I'm kidding. If a place like that *does* exist, I don't know where."

"New rule," I said. "I choose the restaurant. Deal?"

"Deal."

Naked underwear models. Padded bras.

It was almost like Troy was a real person behind his bigwig moneybags persona.

The thought of Troy as a person stuck with me as we

headed out of the office and said goodbye to Lena, who still had a squirt bottle sitting on the corner of her desk. When Troy wasn't being an asshole or trying to woo me with his money, what was he like?

And more importantly, why did I care?

———

WE FOUND a mom-and-pop burger joint off the strip with red vinyl booths and records hanging on the wall. By then, I'd taken off my jacket and tie, not wanting to stay in business attire for any longer than I had to. Troy, who looked like he'd been born in his suit, hadn't so much as undone the top button of his shirt.

The monster.

"You know this place?" Troy asked once we were settled and the waitress had taken our orders.

I shook my head. "Nope."

"It's cute." He pointed across the restaurant. "They have a jukebox. Think it works?"

I looked over my shoulder at where he was pointing. The jukebox was up against the wall near the hostess station, its songs listed through a rounded glass compartment at the top. Tubes lined the corners of the glass compartment, somehow filled with a blue liquid and a yellow lava lamp type substance that rose and fell, growing and splitting apart on a whim. With all of its lights on and the lava lamp part operational, I was pretty sure the mechanics inside had to work, too. "Probably. But I bet all it plays is Elvis."

"Really?" Troy raised an eyebrow. "We're not on the Strip anymore, you know."

"Why don't you go see?"

I didn't expect him to bother with it, but to my surprise, he climbed out of the booth we were seated at and made his way to the jukebox. He looked so out of place there, with his expensive shirt creasing as he leaned down to peruse the song list, that I couldn't help but smile. Was he here just because I'd wanted to eat burgers?

Troy squinted at the machine and spent a short while inspecting it, then moved out of sight in the direction of the cash register. Half a minute later, he returned and pushed two quarters into the slot, then hit two of the jukebox's square buttons. By the time he made it back to the table, my head was in my hands.

"What?" Troy asked as he sat.

"Beat It?" I asked, looking up at him. He grinned at me.
"Really?"

"You wanted me to prove it wasn't all Elvis. MJ isn't Elvis."

I narrowed my eyes. "And you expect me to believe that the only Michael Jackson song on the jukebox was the one with the most suggestive title?"

"It was either this or *Don't Stop 'Til You Get Enough*, and I was pretty sure I'd be in trouble either way."

"Oh my god."

Troy laughed. His eyes filled with emotion, and as much as I didn't want to, I kept finding excuses to look into them again and again. When he wasn't crippling himself on the business front, he was funny.

He opened his mouth to reply, but before he could, our waitress arrived. She slid a strawberry milkshake topped with a generous portion of whipped cream across the table to me, and set Troy's lemon water in front of him.

"I'll be right back with your meals, gentlemen," she told us, then was gone.

"So..." Troy craned his neck to look at the jukebox. "Now

that the Elvis jukebox question has been answered, how was your first day in the office?"

I contemplated his question while I sipped at my milkshake. "Good, all things considered. I'm tired as all hell from jet lag and from how late I stayed up yesterday, but it's been good to see that you're so receptive to the plans I've put forward. I honestly didn't think it was going to turn out this way."

"Neither did I," Troy admitted. "I had no idea what to expect after you sent me that text, and I certainly didn't think you had the business know-how to pick apart our practices and build them back up from scratch. I know you said that you've helped your brother with his business in the past, but... how did you get started? That's not typically something most people just walk into."

"Are you interviewing me?" I raised an eyebrow.

Troy shook his head. "No. I'm curious."

I crossed my arms on the table and turned my head to look at the wall. The salt and pepper shakers were shaped like tiny microphones. I slid the pepper next to my milkshake and turned it in circles, observing it from all sides so I didn't have to look at Troy.

We were supposed to have gone out to eat as work friends, not as a date... but the questions Troy was asking straddled the line between business and pleasure. I guess it shouldn't have surprised me, since as his Dom, my connection to him straddled business and pleasure as well.

"Our dad owned a business," I said simply. "When we were young, my brother and I used to hound him with questions about it. You know how it is when you're small, right? Your dad is the coolest person in the world, and you want to grow up to be just like him."

Troy made no comment.

"So I learned from him. Just little things, you know? The kind of stuff you usually wouldn't know as a kid. Nudge theory, adverse selection, and the curse of first—" I looked up at him and pointed a finger in a joking way in his direction, "—which is handy right now, actually, because that's exactly what you're suffering from at the moment, aren't you? You've developed a lead, and now you're letting your hubris destroy you. Bit by bit, of course, instead of all at once, but it's still the same thing. The principle still applies."

My lips twitched to the side, and I looked at the pepper shaker again. *Beat It* ended, and a second song came on. I didn't know the title, but I knew from the crooning voice that it was Elvis.

I shot Troy a look. He snickered.

"I figured you'd like to know that there *were* a few Elvis songs available," Troy said, grinning. "I couldn't help myself."

"You're a monster."

"Only if monsters have good taste in music." Troy paused for a moment, and his expression turned from playful to serious. "What happened to him? Your father, I mean. Why aren't you running the company with him right now?"

"He died when I was a teenager." I closed my mouth and ran my tongue over my top teeth, trying to hold back the bad memories talking about that time brought up. "It was sudden. One morning, he was at the kitchen table and told Mom he wasn't feeling well. He finished his coffee, took out the garbage, and came to sit back down, but he was fidgety and pale. Mom asked him if he'd call out for the day and go back to bed—sleep off whatever it was—but by then, he was out of it, and he folded his arms on the table and put his head down. He, uh, he never sat back up again." I swallowed the lump in my throat. Even all these years later, it was hard to think about. "He had a heart attack, and they couldn't bring him back."

"I'm sorry."

"You weren't the plaque clogging his arteries." I laughed in an attempt to dispel the sorrow. "It's okay. Death happens, you know? You never want it to happen so young, but sometimes that's just the way it goes. He had a will, of course, but both my brother and I were too young at the time to inherit the company, so it was sold. After paying off all the tax burdens, and the house we were living in, and a university education for me and my brother, we used what was left to start our own business. Even after Dad died, we'd done our best to learn everything we could, from joining the high school entrepreneurs' club to researching on our own after school. As Mills kids, we have a competitive streak, and it gave us an edge."

"But then you left to count cards and work for Rent-a-Dom," Troy said. "Why?"

"Wouldn't you like to know..."

The waitress returned with our food, so I set the pepper shaker back in place near the wall and prepared to chow down. I'd opened up to Troy more than I'd thought I would, and I knew it was dangerous to go any further into detail. I was here as his Dom, and I was here to get revenge on someone who'd wronged me long ago. I wasn't here to make friends, or for him to take pity on me.

"So," I said as the waitress placed my plate in front of me. "About your current staffing situation—here's what I was thinking..."

14

TROY

*R*obin talked until our plates were picked clean and there was nothing left but the foamy pink froth at the bottom of his glass. All of his opinions were well informed and insightful—not only did Robin have business theory backing him up, but he was able to approach his strategies from the viewpoint of someone who, for a period in his life, had done his best to outperform the game and take casinos for all they were worth. It was insight I'd never thought to ask for. Even though part of my security team contained several ex card counters, they'd never suggested any of the work-arounds Robin had suggested.

When I'd pointed that out, Robin flatly informed me it was because I wasn't paying them enough to make it worth it. He'd made note of payment structure from the ground up in his reconstruction plans, too.

It was enough to turn the tips of my ears red from shame.

As a Sullivan, I'd been brought up to make smart decisions and maximize profit wherever possible, but Robin made me doubt that the decisions I'd made were the soundest. There was value in approaching business from a different angle, and while I knew better than to trust blindly in new methods, I had a feeling that if I listened to what he'd said, I'd see astronomical growth.

"So," Robin said. He stretched his jaw from side to side, then scrunched his nose. "I've officially talked so much my jaw is sore."

"I liked what you had to say."

"I'm glad, because you're going to be hearing a lot more of it over the coming months while we roll out phases of implementation."

Changes like Robin was suggesting would need to be passed by the board, but with a little fine-tuning and a well-thought-out presentation, I was sure they'd pass. Step by step, we'd transform The Palisade from the inside, increasing profits and making bold, aggressive moves in order to dominate our market share. The fact that I wasn't forced to go through the planning and process alone meant more to me than I could tell. As Master, Robin had controlled my accounts and made me want to achieve greater things, but as Robin, he'd taken me by the hand and guided me toward greatness.

I could only imagine what new levels of success I'd rise to, now that he was in my life.

"You look like you're thinking about something," Robin remarked.

I blinked back to awareness and shook my head. "Not really. At least, not anything too exciting. I was thinking how grateful I am to have you here, guiding me through this difficult time. I really didn't expect to receive help like this. I was sure that I'd be on my own."

"Oh." Robin paused. Hesitation flashed in his eyes, then disappeared behind his cocky mask. When he spoke again, it was in the dark, sultry way that Master always did. The notes of his voice made my heart race. "I told you that I'd teach you how to take care of yourself, pet. I wouldn't promise you something I couldn't follow through on, now would I?"

Each throbbing beat of my pulse shot downward into my groin. My cock started to stiffen. It didn't matter that we were in a public place and anyone could overhear what we were talking about—I had to obey. "No, Master. I know you wouldn't."

"You're just lucky I'm so understanding. Most Masters wouldn't be so kind, you know." He stretched like a cat, extending his arms far over his head. I watched his slender body elongate itself. Even without his jacket and tie, he was stunning. "But, all things considered, I was impressed with you today. Not only did you listen to me, but you were bold enough and wise enough to point out flaws in my proposal and offer alternatives. I'm exhausted, like you already know, but now I'm wondering if I shouldn't reward you for being so good today... hmm."

The tight warmth of his hole and the touch of his soft, smooth skin came back to me all at once. My heartbeat quickened, and heat burned through my cheeks. I wanted to beg him for a reward, but I knew better than to speak without permission when Master was in the room. I would behave, I would listen, and, if I deserved it, I would be rewarded for my behavior.

"We've still got to pay for dinner tonight," Robin mused. "I wonder if we go to the front to pay. The waitress hasn't stopped by with our bill..."

My hand dug into my back pocket in a flash, searching

for my wallet. I was a second away from standing up when Master reached across the table and grabbed me by the wrist, keeping me from moving. Confused, I looked across the table at him. The dark expression on his face told me that moving another inch was a bad idea.

"What are you doing, Troy?" Master asked.

It was a direct question, so I was allowed to speak. "I'm going to pay for our meal..."

"With what money?"

I pressed my tongue against the roof of my mouth, trying to distract myself from the rush of arousal flooding my veins. When Master was on the other end of the phone, it was easy to forget that my money was his money. When he took what he wanted, I was never there to see it in person—I got to witness it through bank statements and the pictures he sent me. Shopping trips on my dime, fancy dinners paid for by me, new electronics, underwear, suits...

But now, Master was here. The temporary high I felt knowing that I was funding his lifestyle wasn't so temporary anymore. With him there in person, I wouldn't be able to go spend the money in my account on a whim like

I usually did, because that money now belonged to him, and he was here to supervise it.

The staff was going to think I was smuggling a footlong out in my pants, I was so hard.

I had all the money I could ever want, but I couldn't use it. I was powerless to Master's whims.

"You'll come with me," Master told me. "I want you to watch as I spend your money, Troy. Or should I say, my money? Because that's what it is, isn't it? Everything in your account belongs to me."

"Yes," I whispered, hoarse.

"And that's why you're going to do your best to implement the changes we've discussed today, right?" Master held my gaze. Chemistry sparked thick and heavy between us, crushing my lungs like I'd dived too deep underwater. God, did I want him. The feeling was even more intense now that I had him here with me in real life. "I want a fatter bottom dollar, and I want you to do it for *me*."

I shivered. It was embarrassing to do it in front of him, but I couldn't stop myself. How was it that one man was able to take me from zero to one hundred at the drop of a pin? I'd never been so turned on by someone in my life. "Yes, Master."

"Such a good pet." He smirked, then stood and nodded toward the front counter. "Now, come stand behind me while I pay. I want you to see me spend the money. Won't that be a treat?"

I didn't know what I'd done to be so lucky. Master was a dream, and Robin... Robin was something else. Intelligent, funny, informed, and interesting, I felt like I'd never get bored. And with his dominant side coming out to play every now and then, I couldn't get enough.

No omega I'd ever been interested in could compare. Not a single one. Monty had matched me with a man able to steal not only from my casino, but from my heart as well.

I followed Master to the front of the restaurant and stood several steps back so I could watch as he paid. His credit card—one linked to my account, and authorized for use under his name—passed hands, and I watched, rapt, as the cashier rang up the order and swiped the card. At twenty-five dollars including the tip, the expense was minimal and wouldn't even register as a blip on my account, but the act of watching as someone else spent my money and took control away from me entirely hit me hard.

Master was in control now. Without him, I was nothing.

"Come, Troy," Master said casually. He'd already thanked

the cashier and had moved on to exit the restaurant. "Your driver isn't going to want to be kept waiting, is he? He's been very patient this entire time. Maybe I should tip him..."

I bit the inside of my lip to keep from moaning. Master knew exactly what to say to make me feel fantastic. The more he reminded me that he wasn't intimidated by my power or my wealth, the more I wanted him. He could spend every penny of my fortune, and I'd still covet everything he was.

In small but significant ways, he made me human.

I followed him out of the restaurant and across the parking lot to our parked car. Dinner may have been over, but I had a feeling that our night had yet to begin.

15

ROBIN

I walked out of the diner in complete control of Troy, and I arrived at his estate with him wrapped around my little finger. With a few words and gestures, I'd been able to bring a man who thought himself my superior into a state of submission. I'd watched as the confidence evaporated from Troy's face, leaving lust and a total desire to be dominated in its place. It was an easy switch, like flicking on a light, and that I could bring it out of him without much effort was as humbling as it was empowering.

Troy trusted me, someone he'd known on a long-distance basis, but had never met in real life until a few hours before, to guide him. Not everyone could give of themselves so readily. Submission was an act of faith, and whether that meant allowing another person to bring pain or pleasure, or granting someone access to sensitive documents and accounts so they could make life-changing decisions, it was not to be taken for granted.

Once we were through the gates and down the long driveway leading to Troy's impossibly large modern home, Troy exited the vehicle, waved off the driver, and opened the car door for me himself. I got out in silence, taking in the sights. A rock garden stretched along the front of the house, small desert plants artfully positioned within it. The house itself was angular and flat, reminding me more of a Californian home overlooking the ocean than a Vegas paradise. The place was lit up, inside and out, tasteful inlaid lights illuminating each side of the driveway like a classy landing strip. The curtains were open, and through floor-to-ceiling windows, I saw a minimalistic living room. Despite how sparse its furnishings were, they were tasteful and expertly arranged.

"Show me inside," I instructed.

Troy obeyed.

We headed through the front door, past a gruff-looking security guard with dark hair who was far from hard on the eyes, to Troy's bedroom. I'd seen glimpses of it before in the pictures Troy had sent me during play sessions, but seeing it in person was nothing like the glimpses I'd seen. The back wall opposite the door was entirely made of glass and overlooked a rarity in Vegas—grass. Troy maintained a lawn. To the right were two doors, one leading to a master bathroom, the other to a walk-in closet, and to the left was the bed. A royal blue blanket was folded at its foot, its sheets a lighter, refreshing blue so carefully laid that I didn't see a single wrinkle. If I hadn't known better, I would have thought they were painted on. Light, bright hardwood floors and white walls made the room cheery.

Of all the things in the world I would have called Troy even a few days back, cheery wasn't one of them—but it fit him. I was oddly impressed by the space he'd made for himself. Maybe it was the fact that I was in total control of a powerful man, or maybe it was the ego boost knowing that I had the brains and know-how to compete in business with the best of the best, but I felt fantastic. Troy's training would go smoothly if he kept up behavior like this. Even though he was dopey and stubborn, I could make a modern businessman out of him yet. Once he kicked his old habits and saw beyond his stunted viewpoints, he'd rise up and become a force to be reckoned with, and I was going to be the one to get him there.

Me.

Excitement swirled through me, filling my chest and inflating my lungs. Every breath I took was crisp, and it wasn't just the building's incredible central air to blame. In Troy, I'd found another shot at life. For the last three years, my focus had been narrowed on making sure Mom had enough money for chemo and surgery, but now that she was in remission and able to function on her own, I was *free*.

Now that my hands were untied and my resources were limitless, Troy would be my first masterpiece... and while I elevated him to astronomical heights, he would grovel at my feet and kiss my toes one by one, begging me for more.

I needed him. I needed him *right now*.

"Get on the bed, pet." I grinned, the power a rush I wasn't prepared for. Troy was *mine*. "I want to play."

ONE PIECE of clothing at a time, I ordered Troy to strip for me. His belt strap separated from its buckle, buttons parted from button holes, and zippers fell. The fine suit he looked like he'd been poured into hit the floor, puddles of forgotten fabric. When he was nude, I took him in for the first time, letting the sight of him wash through me.

Dark hair with a speckling of white around his temples. Dark eyes. A wrinkled brow and skin thickened by years in the sun. My eyes crept down his neck to his broad shoulders, then to the hair on his chest—salt and pepper. Troy was in shape, and while he wasn't the rippling wall of muscle his bodyguard was, he had nothing to be ashamed of. His body tapered in at the hips, tight and toned. And his cock? Well, I was proud to call it *my* cock. It wasn't outrageously large, but it was thick, and I remembered how it had almost split me open when I'd taken it yesterday.

Why hadn't I wanted to do this again? Being hangry really did strange things to my brain. For a body like Troy's, I would do all kinds of questionable things.

But, for now, his body would have to wait. I came first.

"Make room," I told him. He was sitting on the bed, his cock stiff and standing at attention, weeping precum for me. As much as I wanted to straddle his lap, I wanted to tease him a little first. It was important he remembered his place.

Troy moved to the foot of the bed. Once he was settled and his eyes were back on me, I stripped down, casting aside my clothes. When I was nude, I climbed onto the bed and made myself comfy at its center, belly down, and rested my head on one of his many pillows. My cock was as stiff as his was, now trapped between my body and Troy's fine sheets.

"Come here, Troy," I ordered. While he moved closer, I closed my eyes and smiled to myself. It was time to see how far my loyal pet would go. "I have a treat for you. Tonight, you're going to worship my ass. I want your tongue on me, pet. I want to feel how wet you can get me."

The bed shifted again as Troy moved into position between my legs. He nuzzled his way into the valley of my ass, the stubble on his jaw rough against my cheeks. The warm, wet insistence of his tongue a second later made up for my discomfort—pleasure pulsed through me, and I had to hold back a moan. A tongue wasn't supposed to feel that good, but *fuck,* did it feel wonderful.

Over and over, Troy stroked my hole, sometimes putting pressure, sometimes not. The warm wetness of his tongue turned me on more than I'd thought it would, and I lifted my hips and spread my legs to give him better access. The urge to buck and thrust built up inside of me, and as it did, so did another, familiar feeling—I wanted to be filled.

"Fuck me with your tongue, Troy," I ordered. "Push it deep into me. Wanna feel it, baby."

With a low moan, Troy did as he was told. His thick tongue invaded me, flicking and twisting, until I couldn't take it anymore. I bit his pillow to hold back a scream of pleasure and pushed against his tongue, wanting it deeper, needing it to go *harder*.

"Not enough," I gasped. I wasn't sure if Troy heard me or not—my voice was muffled by the pillow. "Oh, *fuck*, it's not enough. Fuck me. *Fuck me*."

Troy's tongue withdrew. I groaned in dissatisfaction, but the next moment, I heard a wood drawer slide open, then the familiar click of a lid snapping open. In a moment, Troy was back over me, his hips pumping. It was savage, primal, *filthy*, and when Troy's lubed cock finally found my hole and sank into me, how much I needed it almost broke me.

"*Yes*," I hissed into the pillow. While Troy brutally took me from behind, I pushed back against him, working my ass to the timing of his frantic thrusts. "Oh, *fuck* yes. More. *More!*"

The bedsprings squeaked, and the headboard knocked against the wall. I grabbed onto its slats, holding myself steady as Troy gave me everything I needed.

"Master," Troy uttered. He spoke against the back of my

neck, right where the fine hairs at the base of my skull grew. "Please let me come. I need to put it inside you. I need to give you what belongs to you."

Pleasure flashed through me, blinding me to anything else. Troy's cum—*my* cum—needed to be inside me. It needed to be in me as far as it could go, filling me up, so wherever I went, Troy would be there, too. I wanted him to know that I owned what was in his balls, in his bank account, in his head... all of it. I needed *all* of it.

"Come," I demanded. "Fucking come in your master, Troy. Give him what he wants."

Troy let out a choked moan and bucked forward, instantly spilling inside me. If I'd thought his tongue felt good, his orgasm was ecstasy. I bucked back against him and gasped, wanting everything I could get. My own balls clenched, and soon enough, I let go. I shot into Troy's sheets, dirtying myself in the process.

It didn't matter. I'd never been so happy.

"Pet," I panted. "Oh, pet..."

Troy pushed in another time, then let a long while elapse before pushing in again. My spent cock twitched. When Troy pulled out and climbed off me, I got up and pushed him onto the bed, then claimed his lips in a hard kiss that lingered. He kissed me back, matching my passion, and looped his arms around my neck, holding me to him. The more we kissed, the more I wanted from him.

What was getting into me?

"Did I do well, Master?" Troy whispered against my lips.

I smiled. "You did."

And, oh, had he.

We spent the rest of the night exploring each other in bed until, at last, exhaustion got the best of me, and I fell asleep in his arms.

16

TROY

J woke up the next morning better rested than I could recall ever having been, one arm draped lazily across Robin's chest, the other pinned beneath his body. Both of us were nude. Sometime during the night, Robin had pulled the blue blanket up from the bottom of my bed and covered himself with it. It had partially fallen onto me, covering my legs. Now that I was awake, I realized I was way too hot, and kicked it aside, then unwound myself from Robin and slipped from bed.

I'd lost track of the number of times I'd come last night. As Master, Robin was demanding, and my body was ready to perform for him, even though I wasn't the spry twenty-year-old I'd once been. I'd been worried in passing while falling asleep that I'd be too drained this morning to be

useful, but that was far from the truth. Robin's youth rein-
vigorated me, and his greed for my body encouraged me to
keep going. This morning, I felt every bit as young as he'd
made me feel last night, and I was infatuated with him
for it.

I shrugged on a bathrobe and tied the terrycloth belt,
then left the bedroom to head for the kitchen. I took a
bowl from the cabinet and set it on the counter, then
rooted through my fridge for the fresh fruit my personal
assistant made sure was always kept on hand. Strawberries, blueberries, raspberries, blackberries; I brought them
from the fridge and washed them in the sink, then placed
them in the bowl. The strawberries, tiny but incredibly
sweet and flavorful, were a perfect size, and didn't need
to be sliced.

With food at the ready, I returned to the bedroom to find
Robin in the midst of stirring. He stretched out beneath
the blanket and yawned, then cracked open his eyes and
spotted me across the room. Neither of us had thought to
close the curtains, so sunlight streamed in through the
back window and lit everything up. It didn't bother me.
My estate was contained completely within walls, and the
next closest neighbors were distant and behind walls of
their own.

"Good morning," I said as I returned to the bed. I sat at his side, my heart full. "Did you sleep well?"

"Yeah." Robin rubbed his eyes, but didn't make an effort to sit up. "Is it time to get going? We need to get to The Palisade. Shit..."

I set the bowl of fruit on the bed beside him. "Not yet. Let me feed you breakfast."

"Oh?" Robin's voice took on a sultry undertone, and he grinned. "Well, if you insist... feed me, Troy."

One simple command was all it took for me to want him all over again. Holding back from acting on a surge of arousal, I plucked a strawberry from the bowl and held it to his lips. Robin locked eyes with me as he let it into his mouth, then slowly bit down behind the leaves, near where I was holding it from. The fruit disappeared behind his teeth, and I set the green top back in the bowl. A blueberry came next, disappearing behind his pink lips the same as the strawberry had, and then a blackberry. My heart was doing wild, irresponsible things, watching him eat like this.

How the hell could he manage to look so hot eating breakfast? It wasn't fair.

When the bowl of fruit was empty, Robin hummed and

stretched out again. The blanket fell back, revealing his bare chest. I set the bowl aside, then pulled the blanket back and straddled his hips, kissing him deeply. His lips and tongue tasted sweet, and I indulged in them again and again.

"Fuck," Robin uttered during a break in our kiss. "You're making me hard again, Troy. Since when have you ever been so bold? If you're not careful, I'll have to punish you, and we don't have time for that right now—we've got to go to work. There's too much to do to lounge around in bed and fuck all day."

"I can be quick," I promised, my excitement building. Last night had been wild, but this morning would be something entirely different. There was something about the warmth of the sunlight that sweetened the moment. This morning, I didn't want to have sex with Master—I wanted to have sex with Robin. Eager, I started to rock my hips, brushing our groins together.

Robin moaned, then shook his head and pushed me away. "You're so irresponsible when you're horny, pet—it's a good thing you have me here to tell you no."

Our kiss was broken, but I hadn't given up hope. I nuzzled my way beneath his jaw, planting tender kisses on his neck. Having a little fun this morning wouldn't make us late for work provided we stuck to one orgasm each. If I could just get him in the mood...

"No," Robin said firmly. He grabbed my hair and guided me back. "Go take a shower and get dressed, Troy. You'll need to make a stop at my condo so I can change for work today. I will *not* wear the same clothes I did yesterday. Lena's already found a reason to bust out the squirt bottles once."

I smiled. "You have a point."

"Of course I do." He gave me one last kiss—a consolation prize—then pushed me away and rolled over, bringing the blanket with him. "Now go shower. I'm going to find another bathroom and do the same."

"Follow the hallway out the door, third door to the left."

"Thanks." He arched a brow. "Doesn't excuse you from showering. Now, go on. Get going. Don't make me punish you over something so trivial."

After last night's reward, I didn't ever want to be punished again. Happily, I left the bed and went to go wash up. While I knew that Robin wouldn't be coming home with me every night, to know that taking him home was a possibility was incentive enough to behave.

Once the shower was running and the bathroom fan was on, I braced my hands on the sink, looked at myself in the mirror, and laughed. I was *glowing*.

One day, I would make Robin mine. How could I not? A man who made me feel this good about myself was one I wanted to keep in my life. No matter how long it took, or how difficult it was, I'd prove to Robin that I was worthwhile.

17

ROBIN

A month and a half is both a long time, and not much time at all. Six weeks following my takeover of The Palisade, Troy had managed to put together a winning presentation and had presented it to the board. Implementation of the new plan was only just starting to roll out, and it would be a long, arduous process, but that it was being put into action was fantastic. I'd made plans to stick around The Palisade for a few more months, at least until at least the new year, or maybe longer, if I was needed.

After that...

I hadn't given it much thought. There were still a few months ahead of me, and with Troy's wallet at my disposal, I wasn't exactly strapped for cash. I'd worry about my next adventure when I got there. For now, it was nice to settle into a routine, even if that routine was temporary.

I'd made use of my time in Troy's office, of course. After the first few days, I'd eased him into a schedule and made my expectations known. Every morning, whether I'd spent the night with him or not, he brought a coffee to my desk. At one o'clock every day, he delivered lunch to me. I'd expected him to start to slip after the first week or two, after the excitement of having me in town had died down, but to my surprise, he continued to be every bit as submissive and well-behaved as before. I rewarded him generously for it.

On this particular day, at one o'clock sharp, Troy returned to the office with today's lunch offering—grilled chicken Caesar wraps. I'd requested them specifically, so even though he came in carrying a brown paper bag, I knew what was inside. He had a drink caddy in his other hand. I assumed Lena had opened the office door for him, because it looked like there was no way he would have gotten in on his own.

Without a word, Troy came to my desk and set the bag and the drink caddy down. He freed the first paper cup from the cardboard base and set it beside me, then opened the bag to get my wrap. I hadn't exactly been hungry, but all of a sudden, my stomach twisted in the sharp, almost nauseating way it did when it had been left empty for too long. I squirmed in my chair to try to stop the feeling.

"Chicken Caesar wrap, as requested, Mr. Mills." Troy undid the folded top of the paper bag and took out the first wrap. As he did, my nausea spiked. I pushed back from the desk and staggered to my feet, repulsed by the smell.

"Robin?" Troy asked hesitantly as I backed away from the desk.

"Can't..." I was going to puke. I fucking loved chicken Caesar wraps, but this? This musty, tangy smell? It was sickening. "F-Fuck..."

"Robin?" Troy's concern grew. "What's going on?"

"Need to go." I staggered around the desk to the door, then yanked it open. Lena glared at me from her desk. The squirt bottle still sat there, within reach.

"Robin!" Troy yelled after me.

But I couldn't stop. I bolted from Lena's reception area, then down the hall to the bathroom. I managed to close and lock the door, then sank to my knees in front of the toilet and waited for my breakfast to come back up for a visit, or for my stomach to settle.

Not even half a minute later, there was a knock at the door.

"Robin?" Troy asked, more concerned than before. "Are you okay?"

"Did it look or sound like I was okay back in the office?" I asked sarcastically. How many people had put their asses on the toilet seat I was stationed in front of? If I rested my forehead on it, how gross would it be? Was I feeling sick enough that I didn't care? I glanced at the seat, and while it looked clean, I decided I wasn't quite there yet.

"Let me in."

"Are you insane? This is a bathroom."

"I can help."

I took a deep breath that only made me feel sicker and glared at the door. "Unless you have ancient vomit-extracting techniques, I don't think you can help. I'm okay. I just need to... to take a second and pull myself together, that's all. Go back to work."

Troy paused. "You should take the rest of the day off, if not for yourself, then for the sake of everyone else in the office. If you're contagious, and everyone catches what you have, we'll have a larger problem on our hands than you barricading yourself in the bathroom all day."

My temple twitched. Whenever I felt well enough for it, Troy was going to be punished for saying that. Fuck him.

I let the air out of my lungs and hung my head, more tempted than ever to rest my forehead on the toilet seat. The nausea I was going through right now beat out the worst of my hangry behavior. I was short-fused and irritable. While it hadn't been the most emotional or compassionate statement, Troy was right—we were in a business environment, and if I was coming down with a stomach flu, it'd be better if I went home and quarantined myself.

I hadn't been working on anything important, anyway.

"I'm going to stay here until my stomach is settled, and then I'm going to leave for the rest of the day," I finally replied. "The wrap—" just thinking about it made me ill, "—you can do whatever with. I don't want it. I don't even want to *think* about it."

"Understood."

"I'll text you if I don't end up feeling well enough to come in tomorrow," I said. The cool tile floor soaked through the back of my slacks and chilled my ass and thighs. Maybe, if

I put a layer of freshly dispensed toilet paper down, I could rest my forehead on it and cool down. The thought still grossed me out, but I had no clue what else to do. I felt absolutely miserable.

For a long while, nothing was said. I knew Troy was still standing outside the door, but I was too focused on myself to try to engage him in conversation. If he wanted to be weird and stand outside a bathroom door, listening to me potentially puke, that was his prerogative. Right now, I had to think about me.

"Let me come over tonight after work to check on you," Troy insisted. "I won't stay for long—I'm just worried."

"It's a stomach bug, Troy."

"I'm allowed to worry, aren't I?"

I sighed. The last month and a half had been... confusing, to say the least. Troy was my client, and while I'd decided to spend my new free time in his presence, it didn't mean that I wanted something more from him. I wasn't sure that he got that, though. The way he looked at me, the way he submitted to me, and the way he cared for me...

Lines were starting to blur.

If I let him come over tonight, there would be no excusing

it away as business, or as part of my contractual obligation to him. Troy was kind, and sweet, and thoughtful, but I wasn't really looking for a relationship. I valued the time we spent together, and I often found myself thinking about him when my mind was idle, but that didn't mean much. People thought about their friends, or colleagues, or clients all the time. It didn't mean I wanted more.

Not at all.

And the more I told it to myself, the easier it was to believe it.

"Robin?" Troy asked when I didn't respond.

"I..." With a sigh, I gave in. "Fine. You can come over after work to check up on me."

While I didn't want Troy to get the wrong impression, the thought that he'd go out of his way to make sure I was okay was touching. If it'd make him sleep better at night, then who was I to tell him no? He was being kind, and I owed him a little respect.

Right?

Still uncertain, I glanced at the closed door. I imagined Troy standing behind it, his lips a thin line and his forehead wrinkled in worry.

"I really am okay, though," I said. I hoped it would assuage his fear a little. If I wasn't going to be in the office to supervise, I needed him to focus. If he was distracted over me, that would never happen. "I think I must have eaten something that disagreed with me for breakfast. That's all. Or maybe for dinner last night. My brother took me out, and it wouldn't surprise me in the least if something was off."

Monty and his fucking fancy restaurants. I wouldn't pretend to know what molecular gastronomy really meant, but I was sure that one of the fifteen tiny courses served to us last night could have made me sick. We'd been served seafood in tiny shells while wearing VR goggles that had planted us on a sandy shore, and I'd eaten blindly as part of "the experience." Later, when I didn't feel like I was going to get personal with the toilet, I'd send Monty a text and ask him how he was doing. I couldn't be the only one.

"Let Pierre drive you home," Troy insisted. "I'll give him a call and have him pick you up."

"I can pay for a cab, but thank you." I'd draw the line at being brought home by Troy's driver. While I was touched that he wanted to take such close care of me, I was my own man, and I could take care of myself. I didn't want this to get personal. It wasn't supposed to *ever* have been personal, but I couldn't help the way my spirits lifted when I thought about Troy being so devoted, or how pleased I was to think he'd go out of his way to check in with me. "Go back to work, Troy. I'm okay. Thank you for looking out for me so far."

"You're welcome." Troy paused. "I'll see you later tonight."

I heard his footsteps fade down the hall. When they were gone, I let my head sag. I was exhausted after our exchange. What was I going to do about Troy's feelings?

... and what was I going to do about my own?

18

TROY

*R*obin's condo building was one of several on the same block, all of them light-colored, five-story Spanish colonial structures. The entryway to the foyer stood out from the rest of the building, and on top of its roof I spotted twin gargoyles peering down ominously at passersby below. I keyed in the access code for the front door Robin had given me, then took the elevator to his floor and knocked on his door. Faint, upbeat music played beyond the door, and I took that as a good sign. If Robin were at death's door, I doubted he'd be listening to dance music.

The lock clicked. The door opened. Robin, dressed in a baggy t-shirt and sweatpants, opened the door. His hair was combed back from his face, and he wore long green rubber gloves. The front of his shirt was wet.

I'd been expecting to find him weak and in bed, so seeing him like that stunned me.

"Hello," Robin said awkwardly. "I told you I'd be fine, didn't I? I think it was just food poisoning. I don't feel sick at all."

"What are you doing?" I asked, gesturing at his gloves.

Robin looked where I was pointing. "Oh." He chuckled. "Uh, I was cleaning. I've only been here a month, but somehow the condo is a disaster. It's disgusting."

I looked into the condo from over his shoulder. The floors sparkled, and I'd never seen walls so white and scuff-free in rental housing. The hallway beyond the door was void of clutter or mess. It was hard to imagine that there'd be anything dirty inside when even the hallway looked pristine. "Disgusting?"

"It's... you don't see it?" He looked over his shoulder and gestured vaguely at... something. I supposed it was what he believed to be the alleged disaster. "It's really dirty. I came home and, even though I wasn't feeling well, I couldn't stop noticing all the dust and dirt."

"I'm not sure I see anything..." It occurred to me that, if Robin were really sick, he might be delusional. High fevers could invoke hallucinations. If he was seeing dirt that wasn't there and exerting himself when what he really needed was rest, he'd burn himself out. I didn't want that to happen. "Do you think I can come in?"

"No." Robin bristled. He stood rigidly in the doorway, defiant, and locked eyes with me. "You can't come in."

"Will you humor me, then, and let me check your temperature?"

Some of Robin's anger deflated. His posture loosened, and he glanced down the hall before shaking his head, seemingly to himself. "Fine. I guess you can come in. But stay out of the kitchen—I was just mopping in there."

There was something going on, and whatever it was made me uneasy. I followed Robin into the condo as he stepped back and snapped off his gloves, then closed the door behind us. The song playing on the stereo changed. Robin carried his gloves down the hall to an open doorway, then tossed them through. They flopped onto something hard with a rubbery plop.

"Have you been cleaning since you got home?" I asked cautiously.

Robin headed from that doorway to another, inviting me to follow with a wave of his hand. "Yep."

"You should have been resting," I said as I trailed after him. We entered the living room, where the stereo system was set up. Robin's phone had been left on the coffee table, plugged into the speakers. He woke the screen and stopped the music, then turned off the stereo and unplugged his device.

"Blame my Mills genes," he said with a shrug. "I can't not work, Troy. That's not the way I am. Even if I'm feeling sick, I need to do *something* to keep my mind busy."

"There's always sudoku," I said dryly. Now that he was stationary, I closed the distance between us and took the opportunity to check his forehead with the back of my hand. While he was a little clammy from cleaning, he didn't feel hot. Maybe it really had been food poisoning. Still...

Robin swatted at my hand. "Are you satisfied? I told you that I was better."

"Have you eaten anything? You didn't eat that chicken Caesar wrap."

Robin paled. I was sure that if it got any worse, he'd start to turn green. He shook his head. "Don't even talk about food right now."

If the very mention of food turned his stomach, something was still wrong. Whether it was food poisoning or something more sinister, it kicked my protective instincts into overdrive. Robin was sick, and if he kept wearing himself out, he wasn't going to get better. What he needed was rest. Even if I had to stay all night, I'd make sure he got it.

"You're still sick," I remarked.

"Passably sick," he protested.

"If you're not eating, it's only going to get worse."

He waved a hand frantically, face twisting with displeasure. "Can you please stop with the eating thing? Like, no mention of any of that at all, or I *will* puke all over your fancy polished shoes."

"Will you go rest in bed if I ask you to?"

Robin looked at me like I was insane. "No."

"Then I accept my future punishment." I scooped Robin up into my arms as he gasped and flailed, then carried him from the living room and down the hall in search of the bedroom. I knew that acting out against my master's word would land me in trouble, and that I'd pay for what I was doing, but that concerned me less than Robin's state of health. If he didn't learn to slow down and take care of himself when he needed it the most, he was going to get worse, and I couldn't bear the thought of that happening.

"Troy!" Robin squeaked. He pushed at my chest with his palms. "What the hell do you think you're doing! I'm not a baby!"

"Then you need to man up and take care of yourself."

"Troy!"

I found the bedroom at the end of the hall and carried Robin through the door. While he was tall, he was slender, and I didn't find his weight inhibiting. I laid him on the bed as he glared daggers at me, but, to my delight, he didn't immediately spring to his feet or try to bolt past me. Instead, he stayed in bed.

"I'm not happy," he said.

I smiled. "And I wasn't happy thinking about you working yourself ragged while you're not feeling well. Even if it is food poisoning, you need to give yourself time to recover from it. All the dirt you were talking about? The mess? It can wait for another day. Give yourself the next four or five hours off, then call it a night. I want you better."

The anger on his face lessened. He glared at me, but his eyes had lost their ferocity. "You are getting into so much trouble for this."

"Good." I smoothed a hand through his hair, and as I did, the last of his anger disappeared. He shivered. "If I have to pay the price so you'll take time off when you're not feeling well, I'll do so gladly."

"You're awful." Robin's voice was soft and vulnerable.

"I am," I confirmed.

"I should punish you right now."

"You should," I said with a casual shrug. "I've been very disobedient."

"Strip." He looked up at me with indecision, his full lips pressed together with worry. "If you're going to force me to take time off, then I'm going to force you to spend it with me. I want you to cuddle me while I watch movies on my phone."

"I can do that." Spending time in bed with Master appealed to me more than going home alone did. I tugged my tie loose, shrugged off my jacket, and undid the buttons of my shirt. When I was stripped down to my boxers, I climbed into bed next to him. Robin scooted over and turned onto his side so his back was to me, and I took my space behind him, drawing him to my chest. "Is this okay?"

"Yes." He had his phone in his hand and was scrolling through his Netflix app, looking for something to watch. "I'll tell you if I need you to move. But right now... this is fine."

I rested my head on his pillow and closed my eyes, listening to the tap of his thumb on his phone, and savoring the touch of his skin against mine. If I had to spend every day of the rest of my life in trouble because I cared about him too much to stay silent, I would, and if that meant spending every night holding him while he scrolled through movies, I'd do it. Robin had changed my life for the better and kept me going through hard times. I'd do anything I could to return the favor.

19

ROBIN

"Troy?" I asked, a little more than an hour into the second movie of the evening. He was still behind me, one arm wrapped protectively over my side. All night he'd been erect, his cock pressed against my ass, but he hadn't done anything to address it.

"Yes?"

"I'm bored." I set my phone down and closed my eyes, more tired than I'd realized. Over the last few hours, I'd unwound from the stress of the day, and I was feeling it big time. "I think I've been in bed long enough now that I'm not at risk of getting back up to keep cleaning. If you want, you can go. I promise I'll go right to sleep."

Troy hummed against the back of my neck and shifted his weight. He pressed his lips to my shoulder. "Is that so?"

"Yes." I pushed gently back against him, finding myself craving more of his touch. It shouldn't have felt so good, and I shouldn't have wanted it so much. Troy was a temporary pleasure—it wasn't like I wanted him to stick around.

"I'm not sure that I believe you, Mr. Mills," he said playfully, invoking my last name to make a point. "What was it you said about your genes?"

"My genes are tired as shit," I replied. "And so is the rest of me. I promise, I'm not going to be cleaning by candlelight. Right now, all I can think of is falling asleep."

Troy made a small, contented noise, but otherwise didn't reply. The silence gave me time to think. Since Dad had died, I'd always been working on *something*. Whether it was studying my ass off about everything I could about business, heading to Vegas to go to school and start a company with Monty, or putting my brain to work counting cards so I could afford Mom's ridiculously expensive chemo sessions and the ensuing surgery, I'd never taken time to stop and be myself. I was only twenty-two, but if I kept it up, I was going to be old and frail by the time I was thirty.

Maybe Troy was right. Maybe I should take things down a notch.

Damn him for being insightful.

"Do you still want me to go?" Troy asked after a long silence.

A voice in the back of my mind, the same one that urged me to remember that Troy was a client and nothing more, told me it would be better to tell him to go. My body and my heart, however, begged me to let him stay. How long had it been since I'd had someone to hold me when I wasn't feeling well? Someone to take the pressure off, even if it was only for a little while? Troy was there for me —he *cared*—and that was enough to make me change my mind. "I can't believe I'm saying this, but you can stay."

"Why can't you believe it?" Troy asked.

I rolled my eyes back and resisted a smile. "Oh, I don't know, maybe it's because I never thought I'd be inviting the man who humiliated me three years ago to stay in bed with me."

"There was a reason I did that, you know."

"Is that so?" I tapped on my phone screen to pause the movie we'd been watching. While the volume wasn't maxed, the background noise was distracting, and I wanted to hear what Troy had to say. "What reason could you, a man who makes millions of dollars a day, have to shout at someone like me, who walked away with, what, fifty thousand dollars over the course of two weeks? Maybe even less than that?"

"I knew your ID was fake," Troy admitted. "You were just a kid, not even old enough to legally gamble yet. I thought that if you had a bad enough experience, you'd call it quits. I didn't want you to end up in trouble you couldn't get out of."

I wanted to reply, but I struggled to piece together what to say. All these years, I'd only seen the situation from my perspective. Troy had always been the ignorant, snappy bastard who'd wronged me without cause. All of the other casinos on and off the Strip had escorted me off the premises and politely informed me that if I returned, I'd be trespassing, and would be arrested. That was it. But Troy? He was the asshole who'd screamed in my face, who'd threatened me, and who'd put on such a show that I'd never forgotten it.

To think that he'd meant to help me back then, even if his attempts had been misguided...

I exhaled slowly, letting myself depressurize.

"Do you know why I was counting cards and hopping casino to casino?" I asked at last.

"No."

"My brother and I had just spent the remainder of our inheritance on our startup and college tuition. Mom, who hadn't worked in almost two decades, had just started work in retail when she got sick. Really sick." The memory stung, especially after how ill I'd felt earlier that day. "We'd lost our insurance after Dad passed, and the coverage she had at work wouldn't kick in until the six-month mark, and even then, it was shitty at best. But it turned out that didn't matter, because by the time they figured out what was wrong, she'd already been let go from her job. It turned out she had cancer, and we had no way to afford treatment. I dropped out of college and signed over my share of the company to Monty so I could find a way to make the money she needed to get better. Card counting was the only way I could make the money we needed in time to get her the treatment that would save her life."

Troy said nothing, but he didn't need to speak to express his guilt. It hung in the air between us, thick and uncomfortable.

"She's okay," I told him, hoping it would help him feel

better. "I raised the money I needed to, then went home and took care of her while she went through chemo and surgery. It was hard for a while, but she was a warrior, and she got through. She's been in remission for months now, getting stronger by the day, and I left her with enough money to make sure she can get by. So, just so you know, I wasn't some teenage punk beating the system just because I could—I did what I had to in order to save my family. I'm sure you would have done the same."

Troy's arm tightened around me. He pressed a kiss against the back of my neck. "I didn't know."

"Of course you didn't." I snorted. "It's not like I rolled into the pit, slid into a chair at the blackjack table, and announced my mom had cancer. Just... everyone has their story, you know? Even the bratty kid with the big brain taking a chunk out of your profit one discreet sum at a time."

"If I'd have known—"

"Don't." I took hold of his hand and traced his knuckles one by one with my thumb. I didn't want to dwell on the past. While there were always lessons to be learned from what came before, right now, all I wanted to do was look forward to the future. Mom was better, Rent-a-Dom was successful, and Monty was happy with his station in life.

After so long spent caring for others and living selflessly, I was free to be me, and I was happy, too. "Tomorrow is a brighter day, right? I'll feel better, we'll get back to work, and it'll be just like it was before. I'm not any different than I was a few minutes ago, you know—you just know more about where I'm coming from."

"And a little bit more about how to take you to where you want to be."

I turned my head to look over my shoulder, but Troy was lying in such a way that I couldn't see him. Still, the tone of his voice got to me. It had been so tender and sweet, like my path was one he wanted to share with me. I'd never had someone speak to me like that before, and it weakened me to him that much more.

I wasn't supposed to be feeling this way—I'd come here to punish him and satisfy my need for revenge. But when he held me like this, and spoke words that sank straight into my heart...

"Stay tonight," I murmured. "I'm not up for sex, so don't expect any, but..."

Troy chuckled. "I'm not here for sex. I'm here for *you*."

The sentiment behind those words was impossible to fake —Troy *meant* it.

"Troy..."

"You should get some sleep," Troy said softly. He rolled out of bed and headed for the door. "I need to wash up, but I'll be back soon. If you fall asleep before I get back, goodnight, Robin. Thank you for sharing tonight with me."

My heart was fuller than I ever recalled it being. Burdened with feeling, I managed a meager, "Goodnight."

I didn't fall asleep by the time Troy returned, fresh from the shower and mouth minty clean. I didn't fall asleep after he climbed into bed beside me and drew me delicately into his arms, either. There was too much to think, to process, and to feel.

I was falling for Troy Sullivan.

Monty was going to laugh his fucking ass off when he found out.

20

TROY

The room was still dark when the blanket and sheets were ripped from me, and the bed rocked so violently that I woke up in a panic, sure that the bedframe was collapsing. Footsteps bolted across the bedroom floor and the bedroom door was thrust open. Through the dark, I saw Robin dart down the hall and out of sight. Before I had time to process what was going on, I was on the move, too. I jumped out of bed and followed, overly aware of my pounding footsteps in the otherwise quiet condo.

"Robin?" I called out, unsure of where he'd gone. "*Robin!*"

A *thud* sounded in the bathroom, and I rushed toward it, praying that Robin hadn't fainted.

He hadn't—I found him on the bathroom floor, kneeling in front of the toilet. He'd been in such a hurry, he hadn't even turned on the light. Fearing the worst, I dropped to my knees beside him and placed a comforting hand on his back. How long did food poisoning last? It pained me to see him suffer.

Robin's whole body tensed, and his shoulder blades pinched together. He retched, cussed under his breath, then retched again.

"It'll be okay," I promised. "Get it out. You've got this."

"I do... do *not* have this." Robin spat to clear his mouth, then sat back on his haunches. His chest rose and fell heavily. "I am so far from having this it's not funny. I feel awful."

"Do you still think it's food poisoning?" I asked.

Robin glared at me. Moonlight streamed through the small bathroom window, gleaming in his eyes. "Let me just consult the bacteria hanging out in my digestive tract. One sec. Sometimes it takes them a while to answer the phone."

I rolled my eyes—a habit I'd started to pick up from my time with him. "I didn't ask the question to antagonize you. I'm asking out of concern. If you think this is something bigger than food poisoning, I'll bring you to the hospital."

"I'm a jerk. I'm sorry." Robin deflated. "I think I'm hangry again. Hangry, but too sick to eat. You didn't deserve to be snapped at."

"Do you want to go to the hospital?" I pressed. "I'll take you right now. I'm worried about you."

Robin shook his head. "The last thing I want is to sit in a waiting room for twelve hours while I feel like crap, only to be told to take a couple Peptos and head home. I'm fine."

The response didn't satisfy me. It had almost been twenty-four hours since Robin had eaten anything, and while he'd been drinking water, I was worried that he'd dehydrate himself. If a hospital wasn't going to cut it, there were other ways to get him the care he needed. "What if I take you to see my personal physician?"

"It's just food poisoning," Robin mumbled. "I don't see why you're so worried about it."

I rubbed his back. "I'm not worried about it—I'm worried about *you*. If you can't hold anything down and you get dehydrated, then what?"

Robin looked at me blankly. "Then I guess I'll be thirsty *and* grumpy. Thumpy. Thumpy and hangry."

Through force of will alone, I managed not to laugh, but my throat clenched and convulsed, and I knew I was seconds away from losing it. I took a beat to regain my composure, then gave Robin as stern a look as I could muster. "Being thumpy will be the least of your problems. Dehydration can lead to serious health issues."

"I can't take you seriously when you use thumpy in a sentence." Robin wilted to the side, resting his shoulder against the wall. "You're not going to leave this alone, are you? You're going to keep bugging me about it until I give in, even if I order you not to."

"Probably," I admitted.

Robin sighed. "How extremely unfair."

"I know."

"We could bypass the doctor visit entirely by picking up some Pepto. It'll be, what, a couple bucks and half an hour?" Robin looked at me hopefully.

I shook my head. "Nope."

"This blows." The statement was complete, but the last syllable got cut off early. Pale, Robin lurched forward and hugged the toilet, retching again. It broke me to see him so miserable. "... and... and so do I, apparently. Fuck."

"So you'll let me make an appointment?"

"Yes," Robin said without looking up. "Ugh. I feel like total shit."

I squeezed his shoulder. "You won't for long. I'm here now. You've spent so long taking care of others that it's about time someone else took care of you."

AT TEN THAT MORNING, we arrived at the private offices of Dr. Kalia Becker. Robin, who'd managed to sneak in a few more hours of sleep and had woken up feeling better, had argued with me the whole way there, but hadn't ordered me to stop what I was doing. I took it to mean that he appreciated what I did, even if he didn't think it was necessary.

"This is stupid," Robin grumbled. We'd been brought back to the small examination room, and he'd seated himself on one of the chairs. I stood beside him, taking inventory of the posters on the wall. For the most part, they were medical diagrams of the human body—the throat, the brain, the hands—but there were a few about

the spread of bacteria, and another few about the impor-
tance of proper sanitation. "Troy, I've been sick for less
than a day. I know that you're worried, but it's not like I'm
going to keel over. Sometimes, people get sick."

"You were the one who gave me permission to make me
the appointment," I replied as I came to sit next to him. "If
you were feeling sick enough earlier this morning to agree
to it, then something's going on. Humor me."

Robin sighed. "I really should punish you, you know.
You're getting too comfortable with overstepping your
boundaries."

There wasn't a trace of Master in his voice, so I doubted
he meant it, even though it was true.

"I wonder what I should do to you..." Robin tilted his head
back, a hint of a smile on his face. "Maybe I should strip
you down and tie you up in front of the windows of your
office—let the whole world see the great Troy Sullivan
reduced to nothing more than a body. Or maybe, hmm...
maybe that's not enough." A sly tone crept into his voice,
and with his head still tilted back, he glanced at me. "I
own you, you know. Every dollar, every inch of skin, every
hair. I feel like lately, you've been forgetting that." He ran
a hand over my crotch, and my cock hardened at once,

eager for his touch. "I should lock this up and throw away the key for... what? A week? Two?"

My pulse skyrocketed, and I pushed into his hand, wanting more. After the sweetness of last night, it was good to remember that Master still lived in Robin's mind and was eager to come out to play.

"In fact," Robin murmured. The more he spoke, the more he tended toward sultry tones. "I think, when we get home, I'm going to order you to sit next to me and watch while I shop for cock cages with your credit card... and maybe, if I see something else I like, I'll add it to my cart, too. How many toys do you think I'll find? With your cock in a cage, maybe I should put a plug in your ass, too— make you wear it to all your meetings. While I'm at it, I'll get a little vibrator, slip it in there, and leave it buzzing. Mm, *fuck*, Troy..."

Aroused wasn't the right word for what I felt—I was on goddamn *fire*. Heart pounding, pulse racing, I turned in my chair to face him, but before I could say anything, there was a knock on the door. I jumped and spun back around in my chair, hoping Dr. Becker wouldn't notice my erection. My cheeks burned, and I was sure my face was flushed. Robin had to be feeling better—a stunt like that wasn't the kind of thing a sick man had the energy to do.

"Come in," Robin said casually. If it hadn't been for the tiny smirk on his face and the mischief in his eyes, I would have accused him of looking bored. He'd done it on purpose, likely as a way to get revenge for having dragged him to a doctor's appointment. Seeing him playful instead of miserable gave me hope that everything was going to be okay.

The door opened, admitting Dr. Becker. Her short brown hair was styled to look windswept, and she carried herself with a timeless grace that spoke of confidence and intelligence. "Hello, Mr. Sullivan, Mr. Mills."

"Hello, Dr. Becker," I said. "Thank you for seeing us on such short notice."

"I'm glad I could fit you in," she replied. She had a medical chart tucked under her arm, which she glanced at to reference. "It seems today's appointment is for Mr. Mills—Mr. Mills, do you want Mr. Sullivan to stay, or would you prefer I see you alone?"

"He can stay," Robin said. "Really, if he stays in the room and you can convince him it's nothing scary and life-threatening, I'd appreciate it. I have food poisoning, but the way he's acting, you'd think I caught Ebola."

Dr. Becker chuckled. She moved to her desk and set the chart down, then put on a pair of examination gloves and selected a tongue depressor from a sterile container. "I'll be able to tell you pretty conclusively if it's Ebola or not in a second, but based on a quick visual exam, I'm going to say you're fine."

Robin arched a brow victoriously and looked in my direction. I shook my head. "I never said it was Ebola. I just said that I was worried. Dehydration is a valid concern."

"That I do agree with," Dr. Becker said. "Mr. Mills, will you sit on the examination table, please? While you're getting settled, can you tell me about what's been going on?"

Robin got up from his chair and went to sit on the examination table. The paper sheet over it crinkled when he sat. "Yesterday at around one in the afternoon, I got sick. Troy had just brought me lunch, and the smell of it didn't agree with me, and that was it. I went home and felt good enough to get some cleaning done, then settled in for bed and woke up at around three this morning sick all over again. I really do think it's food poisoning. I went to some trendy molecular gastronomy restaurant the other day, and it was probably something I ate there."

"I'm not so certain about that." Dr. Becker came to stand beside Robin. "Mouth open, tongue flat."

Robin did as told, allowing Dr. Becker to get a look at his tongue and throat. She checked his eyes, then hummed thoughtfully and returned to her charts.

"I'm not seeing any overt signs of illness. You're not running a temperature, you're not pale, your eyes aren't bloodshot, and while you do seem to be a little dehydrated, it's nothing a little Pedialyte can't fix. What troubles me is the fact that you felt better between bouts of extreme nausea."

Dr. Becker discarded her gloves and tapped her fingers on her desk. "It could be food poisoning, I suppose. Not everyone manifests symptoms in the same way. I see that your charts mention that you're an omega—could it be possible that you're pregnant, Mr. Mills?"

A single question was all it took for the world to stand still. My chest clenched and my throat closed, and as they did, my mind grew foggy.

Pregnant?

Robin had never asked me to use protection, and I'd never bothered to use it. We'd been having sex at least once a week, and oftentimes more than that, since he'd come to teach me how to take care of myself following the Redding disaster. I'd thought, naively, that he'd have put himself on birth control, but...

"Robin?" I asked in a small voice.

Robin's shoulders were pinched to his neck. "I mean, it's possible," he said stiffly. "I don't think it's likely, but... but, I guess it could be a thing."

"I can run some bloodwork if you'd like. That way, we can rule it out." Dr. Becker looked us both over, her expression kind. She didn't judge us, and for that, I was grateful. "It'll take all of about ten minutes."

"Yeah. Sure. Why not." Robin swallowed nervously. "Once we get it crossed off the list, it'll have to be food poisoning, right?"

"Unless the symptoms don't improve, yes."

"Then let's do it." Robin held out his arm.

I couldn't speak—all I could do was look at him and imagine what could be.

Pregnant?

If he was, he was less than two months along. How many more months would pass before he started to show? Until he grew round with our child, skin glowing, eyes bright? I pictured him like he was on his best days, mischief alight in his expression and his lips pushed to the side in a cocky grin as he held his baby bump with one hand.

Look what you've done now, he'd whisper in Master's honeyed voice. *You're going to have to provide for both of us, Troy. It's going to get expensive, and I'm going to make sure every cent I need comes from your account. Imagine the nursery I'll build. Light, bright, and beautiful. I won't spare a single expense. It's only the best for me and for our child, right? We'll live in luxury while you foot the bill...*

I had to shift my legs to hide the way my cock was tenting my fly. With Master, my rules and hard limits had always been rigidly defined. We'd set budgets and drawn the line when it came to how much he could take from my account in a day, a week, a month, and a year. Since he'd come to Vegas, those rules had been looser than ever, but still existed in some nebulous form or another. But now that there was a chance we had a baby on the way? There would be no more boundaries. Master could dip his fingers as deeply as he wanted to into my accounts—he could drain me for everything I had... and I'd let him do it.

For the rest of my life, I would provide for him—I would provide for *both* of them.

It aroused me at the same time as it gave me hope.

I'd be a *father*.

It had never been something I'd wanted, but now, I craved it more than anything else.

———————

TEN MINUTES HAD NEVER LASTED SO LONG. I sat still and silent in the chair beside Robin, too tense to move, to fidget, and almost to breathe. Beside me, Robin sat quietly, head turned away from me, chin rested in his hand. I didn't take offense. An unexpected pregnancy was an emotional event, and he was entitled to whatever he was feeling. In time, when the news had sunken in, we'd discuss it together and make things right. No matter what, I would take care of him. It had all come on suddenly, but I knew it in my bones, my heart, and my head. Robin was the one I wanted, and baby or not, in face of a potentially life-changing event, I knew beyond a shadow of a doubt that I never wanted to let him go.

Twelve minutes after Dr. Becker had left the room with

Robin's blood sample, she returned. Robin lifted his chin, his face expressionless. "What did the results tell you?"

Dr. Becker closed the door. She offered us a smile. "The blood test came back positive, Mr. Mills—you're pregnant."

21

ROBIN

*P*regnant.

On the silent ride home, I ran my hand over my flat stomach and tried to make sense of what I'd been told. I was *pregnant*. Right this very second, there was a bundle of cells—or at this point, a pea-sized, peanut-shaped alien creature—growing inside of me. A tiny hijacker who belonged to me as much as it belonged to Troy. An irreversible, permanent mark that would always link me to the Sullivans.

It wasn't right.

I glanced at Troy, who was driving. Anticipating he'd stay the night, he'd come on his own to my condo, and he'd driven me to my last-minute appointment with Dr.

Becker. While he kept his eyes on the road, it looked like his mind was elsewhere. There was a small, dreamy smile on his face, and he looked relaxed.

Relaxed.

How could he look peaceful at a time like this? There was a *fetus* inside me, for god's sake. I'd take Ebola over this any day of the week.

Annoyed, I slumped back in my chair and looked out the window. Traffic was heavy, and it gave me a chance to watch the scenery as we passed it by. Tall buildings, shopping centers, hotels, restaurants—even off the Strip, the city was full of life. I rested the top of my head against the window and stroked my flat stomach again, wishing I'd been more careful. Monty had warned me—he'd fucking *warned* me—but I'd been too arrogant to listen.

What was I going to do?

"It's not the end of the world, you know," Troy said softly. The hopeful way he spoke made me want to punch him. "A baby isn't going to change anything."

"For you, maybe," I shot back. I did my best not to snap, but I was nauseous, and hungry, and afraid. Troy wasn't carrying this child, his life wasn't going to be forever impacted by it, and his freedoms weren't going to be taken away. All he'd have to do was sign the checks and call on holidays and birthdays. What was a few-strings attachment for him was an all-strings attachment for me. "For me, it's a really big fucking deal."

Some of the happiness on Troy's face vanished. Guilt spread through my chest and rose up my throat, leaving me as sick as I'd felt this morning. Maybe if he understood where I was coming from, he wouldn't feel so upset. "We're talking about a *baby*, Troy. A real-life, living, breathing, diaper-soiling person. A person who's going to grow into an adult. A—"

"I know what a baby is," Troy said calmly. "I also know that, no matter what, I'm not going to leave you to raise it alone. Even if you want nothing to do with me anymore, I'm going to be there for that child. I'm going to be the best father I can be... and if you let me, I'm going to be the best partner I can be, too."

No.

No, no, no.

No.

I closed my eyes and turned my head to rest it against the window, wishing I could jump out of the car, roll down the bank, and disappear. Troy wasn't the man I'd imagined him to be when I'd met him at nineteen years old, but that didn't change the fact that he was my client. Our relationship was strictly professional. I'd only let him sleep in my bed last night because...

Because...

I curled up against the door and tried not to think about it. Troy was a *client*. I was the one who was confused. I'd let feelings cloud my better judgment, and now we were in too deep. I had feelings for him, yes, but to go from client and service provider to fathers? To life partners? It was so sudden and jarring, it made my head hurt.

If he kept talking, I wasn't going to be able to hold myself together. Right now, I didn't need commitment—I needed time.

"Take me home, Troy," I whispered. "I don't really want to talk right now. All I want is to go home."

"Robin..."

"*Please.*" I'd wanted to sound stern, but my voice broke. I was falling apart at the seams, and nothing was going to stitch me back together but time spent reflecting on what I needed. It was a conclusion I needed to come to alone.

Troy frowned and said nothing after that. We returned to

my apartment, and I mumbled a goodbye before I escaped from the car and hurried inside. I had feelings for Troy, but because of them, I'd made a mistake that was going to change both of our lives. That was my burden to bear, and for now, it was one I needed to bear alone.

Loneliness didn't help. I spent the first few hours lost in cyclical thoughts, obsessing over the same small details until my head throbbed and my heart ached. There was no way out of this. The kind of mistake I'd made wasn't a mistake that could be undone or forgiven. There was another life involved now, and whatever I did, I had to think of it in addition to myself.

But the more my mind kept spinning, the less certain I became.

What was the best way forward? Options unraveled before me like balls of yarn batted across the floor. I could take the baby and go back to Maine, to Mom, and live a normal, quiet life with a child who'd never know his father. I could focus on work and reclaim my spot next to Monty as one of the heads of Rent-a-Dom, guaranteeing my child an easy life with occasional visits from his father.

I could stay with Troy and play the perfect partner, whatever that would mean...

I huffed a sigh and wilted onto the couch, settling so my head rested on the arm, and my legs were stretched across the cushions. Right now, I was too unfocused and fearful to come to a solid conclusion. If I made a decision now, without having taken the time to step back and look at the bigger picture through several critical lenses, I was going to regret it. But at the same time, time was ticking. I'd left Troy on uncertain terms, and I knew it had to be eating at him not to know what I felt. He'd made a declaration of love and faithfulness, and I'd shut down on him.

I really was a piece of work.

With too many options to sort through, fearful and unable to focus, I called the only person I was sure could help— my rock and my cool source of reason, Monty.

"To what do I owe the pleasure of your call, little brother?" Monty asked upon answering.

I scrunched my nose. "Little brother? I'm not all that much younger than you, you know."

"But you *are* still younger." Monty chuckled, but he sounded distracted. Was something going on in his life, too? "I hope you're calling about dinner plans. I was just thinking about sending you a text to ask if you'd go out with me this weekend. There's a great—"

"No." I hadn't meant to cut him off, but I couldn't let him ramble on, either. Feeling guilty, I added, "I'm sorry. I... I'm actually going through something really, *really* big right now, and I need you to help me figure it out. I didn't know who else I could call."

"Oh." Monty's voice was graver than before, burdened with the unknown. "I'm here for you. What is it?"

One beat passed, then two. At last, I let out a shuddering sigh and said, "I'm pregnant."

"Robin..."

Now that I'd said it, I couldn't hold back anymore. I clutched the phone to my ear and curled up on the couch, feeling small and afraid. "It's Troy's. I... we... it's complicated, and I was stupid, and now... now I'm going to have his child, and I don't know what to do. I didn't want this to happen, but I was so caught up in the fantasy that I didn't even... I didn't even *try* to use protection with him. And now I've gone and fucked everything up, and I don't know what to do anymore."

Saying it out loud felt nice, but I hated the weakness in my voice. I was better than that.

"Robin..."

"I'm such a mess," I murmured. Hopelessness prickled beneath my skin and irritated the shit out of me, but I pushed it aside and did my best to keep a level head. I'd already snapped at Troy—I didn't want to snap at Monty, too. "What do I do? I didn't want any of this to happen, but I can't take it back now that it's done. I'm *pregnant*, Monty. I'm not... I'm not ready. I don't know what the fuck I'm doing."

"You could end the pregnancy," Monty suggested.

"No." I couldn't get the word out of my mouth quickly enough. I'd only just learned that there was a life growing inside me, but I already knew that I didn't want it to end.

"Hmm..." Monty's voice took on the contemplative, teasing tone it usually bore. "You didn't even need to think about that one. Are you sure you don't know what you're doing? Because it sounds to me, when you answer so quickly, like you have a plan."

The hairs on the back of my neck stood on end. "Just because I know that I want to keep the baby doesn't mean anything."

"Sure it does," Monty continued. "It shows some degree of foresight. You've decided that you're willing to take responsibility for the new life you've created, and you've already devoted yourself to its cause. You have your foundation. From there, all you need to do is stack the bricks one by one until you finish the job."

I hated how easy Monty made even the most challenging things sound. "It takes a lot of work and time, you know, to put a brick house together. It's not easy."

"Very few things in life worth doing are easy," Monty said. "Hold on one second."

The phone beeped, putting me on hold, but before it did, I heard Monty say, "Choke on—"

When the call beeped again, connecting me directly with Monty's phone, I was too stunned to say anything right away.

"Now, where was I?" Monty asked. "I'd just told you that very few things in life worth doing are easy, right?"

"Are you in a session right now?" I asked, astonished. I knew that from time to time, Monty took on clients, but I hadn't expected him to answer his phone while he was dominating someone.

"I might be," Monty said, evasive as always. "But even if I

am, a conversation with you is more important to me than tending to the needs of any lowlife, filthy pig."

He was in a session—no doubt about it. I made a face. "Monty, *gross*."

"Hey, you're calling to ask for help after you let your sub knock you up. I should be the one calling *you* out."

I supposed he had a point.

"So, here's what I want you to do." Monty kept his voice even and his tone kind. "Start looking at the bricks you have on hand, and if you want to include them in your future or not. Ultimately, it's up to you, but the choices you make will affect the structural integrity of the life you build for yourself. What do you want to do about Troy? Your position within Rent-a-Dom? Your relationship with your family? Start there. Even if you can only decide on what you don't want, you'll be a step closer to knowing what bricks you have left to build with, and what kind of a future you can make with them. Does that make sense?"

"Yes." I uncurled and lay flat across the couch. "I've got to call him, don't I?"

"I think you should," Monty agreed.

"I was kind of an asshole to him, the last time we spoke," I admitted. The guilt I'd felt in the car returned. "He was trying to comfort me, but I was too busy shutting down and freaking out to hear him. Do you think that he'll forgive me?"

"I don't know." Monty paused for effect. "I guess it depends on if you're sincere or not, doesn't it?"

The statement caught me off guard, and I struggled to reply. After a few failed attempts to find words, Monty chuckled.

"I'm going to take it that what I just said might have helped you find your way." Monty paused. "I'm glad. If you need any more help, you know you can call me back, but for now, I'm going to have to let you go. While it's sudden, and frightening, and new, I know what whatever you decide will work out for you in the end. You're the man who gave up everything so he could to help Mom when she was sick, and you still managed to come out on top. No matter what choices you make, or where life takes you from here, I have confidence that you will succeed."

The heartache I'd been carrying lessened. I managed a smile. "Thank you."

"You've got this, Robin," Monty promised. "And if you don't, then you know that *we've* got this. I told you when you came back to Vegas that I'd take care of you. I wasn't lying. If you need me, I'm here for you. I will *always* be here for you. Mom is, too."

"I'm here for you, too," I replied, choked up. "I'm here for you and Mom, always."

"Text me about whether you're on for this weekend," Monty added. "We'll talk again soon."

"See ya."

The conversation ended, but the effect it had had on me remained. Monty hadn't given me an answer, but he had helped direct me toward making the best possible choice. No matter what bricks I used to build my future, I would still be whole. Having a baby would change my life, but it wouldn't end it. In the end, everything was going to be okay.

I pulled up my contacts list and dialed Troy's number. I wouldn't put off our talk any longer. If I was going to make an informed choice about my future, I needed to know where he stood, and if our bricks could slot together.

22

TROY

The twin gargoyles I'd spotted during my last visit peered down at me from above the entryway to Robin's condo building, their stony, unmoving faces twisted with predatory glee. I did my best to pay them no attention, but as crazy as it sounded, I *felt* their eyes follow me. It was like they knew my secrets, and they longed to watch the drama unfold in real time.

I crossed the courtyard more quickly than necessary to get away from their leering faces and entered the code to access the foyer. Heart pounding, I crossed to the elevators and stepped inside, thumbing the button that would take me to Robin's floor. Dread stirred deep in my bones, like my very marrow itself had succumbed to its influence.

The longer I dwelt on it, the more apprehensive I became of the encounter to come.

Robin was an independent, strong-willed young man who knew how to take care of himself. I'd opened my heart to him and let him know that I would be there for him no matter what, but he was more than capable of taking care of himself and our child without me. There was no way I could make him stay... and judging by the despondent look in his eyes and the way he'd fled my car earlier that day, I had a feeling that staying was the last thing on his mind.

If he ended our contract, I'd get over it. If he told me that he'd never be my master again, I would survive. But if he asked me to leave? If he told me he never wanted to hear from me again, and that he was leaving town? It shredded my heart to pieces just thinking about it. I didn't want to lose him, and I didn't want to lose our new family.

But who was I to make him stay?

Terrified of the conversation to come, I stood in front of Robin's door and did my best to gather my courage. I was no stranger to loss. In the blink of an eye, I'd lost tens of millions of dollars—but the crushing sense of foreboding that came from losing a chunk of my fortune couldn't compare to the dark, creeping dread weighing down my soul when I thought about losing Robin. No matter how long I stood in front of that door, I couldn't push that heavy, horrible feeling away.

I went to knock only for the door to open. Robin, ashen faced, stood in the doorway, his eyes no longer mischievous, and his playful energy gone. He stepped back from the door and crossed his arms over his chest, then looked aside uneasily. He'd invited me here, but the look on his face told me that he wasn't happy about it. A hard conversation was coming, and both of us knew it.

"Hey," Robin said quietly. He scuffed his foot on the floor, then tucked his chin against his shoulder and shifted his weight from hip to hip. The more he fidgeted, the antsier I became. "Thanks for coming out all this way."

"Yeah, of course," I said. I'd wanted to keep my voice neutral, if not upbeat, but it was hard to convince the stress I was under to stay out of my voice.

Robin took another small step back, vacating a spot in the hallway beyond the door that I could occupy. "You wanna come in and get settled in the living room? I don't think this is the type of conversation we should have in the doorway, you know? I'd rather we be comfortable."

"Sure." My heart was in my throat, but I did as told. If

nothing else, I was obedient—Master's perfect pet. No matter how muddled the line between personal and professional had become, I was still his pet, his Troy. I would listen until the end.

We headed for the living room together. Robin kept his arms tucked over his chest, and he held himself in ways that seemed to suggest he was uncomfortable in his own skin. In all things until then, he'd always been composed and steadfast—entirely certain of himself. Seeing him like this rattled what little confidence I had left. If the man who so easily dominated me couldn't hold it together, I could only imagine what was coming.

This was it.

We sat on the couch on opposite sides, Robin's shoulders tight and his thighs pressed together. He ran his hands down his sweatpants nervously. "We need to talk. You know. About... what's going on."

I stayed silent. Right now, listening was more important than expressing my emotions.

"I want you to know I'm sorry that I snapped at you before —that I've had such a temper lately. That's on me. You don't deserve to be treated like that, and I'm sorry. No matter what happens, and how many emotions I have to work through, you deserve more respect than I gave you, and I promise, I'm going to try my best not to let it happen again."

The fear clenched in my heart loosened, if only a little. I sat up straighter and looked at Robin more closely, stunned by what he'd said.

"I know that we have a contractual relationship," Robin continued, "and I know that you turn to me as someone you can depend on—someone you can spoil, and care for, and cherish, who won't be mushy for you only because of your money. That means I have to keep up a kind of persona, you know? I *am* Master, and I love the play sessions we have together, but I... right now, I need to talk to you as Robin, and I hope that doesn't upset you or otherwise change your mind about me."

"Of course not." I smiled. "It's not just Master I'm interested in, you know, and as much as I love it when you slip into your role and dominate me, I value you for who you are as a complete individual. For the last little while, you've been more Robin than Master, anyway. It hasn't made me want to run."

A small smile upturned the corners of Robin's lips. His gaze was locked on his knees, but some of the melancholy that had been surrounding him faded away. "You're too stubborn to run, anyway, aren't you?"

I grinned. "Guilty as charged."

"But that's not really what we need to talk about right now." Robin rolled his shoulders back, sucked in a breath, then faced me. Determination burned in his eyes, backed by fear of the unknown. "Right now, I'm talking to you as Robin, about Robin, and about Troy. Over the next few months, I've got to make important decisions about my future, and I need to know... in a perfect world where what you wished for the most came true, what would you want? No matter what you say, you won't offend me. I need to hear the truth."

I looked at him, momentarily at a loss for words. Had Robin believed that my affection was conditional? No wonder he was so torn up. "Robin..."

"I just need to know if you meant what you said in the car earlier today." Robin's fingers curled against his palms, forming loose fists. "If our contract ended tomorrow and I wasn't your Dom anymore, would you want to be there for me? Would you still support me and the baby? I won't think less of you if you say no, but I need to know so I can plan my own future." He set a hand on his stomach. "*Our* future. So, please, be honest."

My words returned, and I used them as best I could. "In a perfect world, your future is my future." I looked in his direction, glad to see the sparkle returning to his eyes. The melancholic aura between us evaporated, and the weight in my chest started to lift. "I don't care if you're Master or Robin or whoever else you'd like to be. I want the contract to end, and I want something more to take its place. I'm not speaking as your submissive when I say I want to take care of you—I truly, honestly do."

Robin's smile grew a touch more bold, and seeing it made me smile in turn.

"If you want to keep overseeing the company, I'd be glad to hire you on as an adviser," I continued. "If you'd rather stop all of that and focus on fatherhood, I will support you all the way. If you never want to be Master again, I won't beg you to consider otherwise. In my perfect future, you're happy with yourself and your choices... and you're happy with me, too."

"You'll take care of this baby?" Robin asked. "I don't want to have to command you to do it, or for you to feel like you're obligated to be there for us. I don't want money to be involved—not like it is during play. All I want to know is if you'll be a father."

"Yes." I said it without hesitation. The thought of caring

for Robin and the baby had excited me before, but that excitement had mellowed and turned into something more profound since I'd parted ways with Robin earlier that morning. What I'd wanted all this time was to be told no—to see that there was someone out there who wouldn't bend to my will simply because money was involved. Robin had given me that escape by taking control of my finances and taking the upper hand in the relationship, but now, with a child on the way, my relationship with the world had changed. As a father, there would be ups and downs. There would be temper tantrums and meltdowns just the same as there would be sweet moments and laughter. I'd have a young life to dote on, to cherish, and to provide for. The money I made wouldn't sit and gather dust anymore—every cent I made had purpose. One day, they'd fund the endeavors of my son or daughter, and any other children that followed.

As a father, I would be normal to at least one young soul.

Two, if Robin chose to stay.

I would work hard for them forever if it meant they would be cared for and happy. While I'd miss it, with them in my life, I didn't need to be dominated. In them, I'd found where I belonged.

"I want to be a father to our child," I clarified, making sure

Robin understood in no uncertain terms. "I want to be a partner to you, too. I'm in this, I'm devoted, and I'll see it through until the end. I *love* you, Robin." I reached out and placed my hand reassuringly on his thigh. "And while this isn't the way I pictured I'd start a family, I know I want this. I know I want *you*."

Robin blinked away tears. "Then I need to tell you the truth."

"The truth?"

"Rent-a-Dom?" Robin swallowed hard. "The contract we established through Monty? I..." It looked like he didn't want to continue, but he powered through regardless. I loved that he was so strong even when in the face of great difficulty. No matter what he said, I would return his courage with my own. "I wasn't exactly a Dom at the time. A while ago, you asked me what I was doing working for the company, and the truth is... I *started* the company, then had to leave it after Mom got sick. Someone had to care for her, and so while Monty focused on recouping our expenses from starting up, I hit every casino I could to raise funds for her treatment."

I stared at him, unable to speak. I'd simply assumed that Robin was a contractual Dom. But if he'd, at one point, been the owner...

"Monty contacted me after you sent in your application because he thought it was too good to pass up, based on our history." He clenched his hands into fists. "I just... I needed you to know everything. I don't want any secrets out there, threatening what we have, if you decide to stay."

"I am staying." I didn't waste a second in replying. Robin was worth more to me than that. If he thought a secret like that would be enough to convince me to leave, he was crazy. My heart was invested. I never wanted to say good-bye. "I meant it when I said I love you. I'm not going anywhere."

He laughed a panicked but deliriously happy laugh, then brushed the tears from his eyes. "I love you, too. I want to find a way to make us all as happy as we can be. Will you help me? I don't have a definitive plan this time around, and I don't know what path is best to take... but I figure that, together, we can figure it out."

I smiled. Joy radiated from my core, soaking through my muscles so I glowed from within. As much as I appreciated the Robin who knew exactly what to do, and who was quick to take control, I loved the Robin who let me in —the one with whom I'd plan our future.

"Seven months should give us more than enough time to

come up with a proposal." I squeezed his thigh. "I think we'll have our lives sorted by then."

Robin laughed, but the sound of it was coarse, and a moment later, it devolved into tears. He launched himself across the couch and wrapped his arms around my neck. I held him loosely and closed my eyes, my heart so full of the moment, I thought it might overflow and bring me to start crying, too.

The way forward wouldn't necessarily be easy. We had a lot to learn about the life we were about to embark on, and about each other. But with drive like ours, strengthened by love and fortified with trust, I knew we'd figure it out.

23

ROBIN

"$\mathcal{M}$r. Mills, sir?" Westward trailed after me nervously as I strolled down the hall, my hands tucked in the back pockets of my dress pants. He struggled to keep pace. If the red, blotchy color of his face told me anything, it was that something was going on, and he was stressed to no end about it. "Mr. Mills, please! Please, wait!"

I decided to entertain him. "Yes, Westward?"

"There's..." Westward glanced down the hall at the door leading into Lena's office, and through it, to the office I now shared with Troy, then trailed off. After a few tense emergency meetings with the board in which I'd swayed them with my cool intellect and sharp wit, I'd been granted an official executive position within The Palisade, and served alongside Troy as we rolled out the changes to The Palisade's staffing and policy structures that would take it from a good casino on the Strip to the *best* casino, period. Over the last few months, I'd worked tirelessly alongside Troy to make sure the implemented changes were living up to expectations, and, if they weren't, that they were promptly revised and corrected.

Troy, bless him, was working harder than ever—and not only that, but he was learning, too. Pregnancy *sucked,* but it had lit a fire under his ass that not even the most intense play sessions had been able to accomplish. The stubborn man I'd met almost five months ago was finally starting to think outside the box. Maybe it was because I was living with him now. Life on the estate made up for how much pregnancy sucked.

Barely.

But more than that, Troy's willingness to grow and learn pleased me an impossible amount, and I was pretty sure he knew it.

"There's?" I asked. I looked down the hall at the same door, which made Westward flail and jump in front of me, seemingly in an attempt to block it from my view. His efforts were wasted—he was too short to hide much of anything.

"There was a situation in the office," Westward stated. The red on his face darkened and grew splotchier. "It's Lena, sir. Do you remember the squirt bottle she's had sitting on her desk for the last few months?"

I snorted with laughter. "Yes."

I'd dodged sprays from that same squirt bottle on my first day here, when Westward and Lena both had been convinced that I was some kind of hooligan looking to cause trouble. From time to time, I still taunted Lena with rubber bands, even though I didn't fire them at her anymore.

"Just now, there was a visitor in the office who acciden-tally knocked the squirt bottle to the floor. The cap came flying off, and the water went everywhere. Until we get it soaked up, can you please wait out here? It shouldn't be long, but we don't want anyone to slip and fall—especially in your condition."

"My condition?" I shifted my weight from one foot to the other, subtly emphasizing the growing baby bump I was sporting. At four and a half months pregnant, I was show-ing. "I always forget how pregnancy makes the bottom of your shoes suddenly much more slippery. Thank you for looking out for me, Westward. Pregnancy brain makes me forget everything all the time. I don't know what I'd do without a little help."

I was teasing him, of course, and I let my playfulness shine through in my words. Westward, bumbling and anxious about everything, wrung his hands and shook his head quickly. "That wasn't what I meant, sir..."

"I know, I know." I grinned. "I'm sorry. I think I must be spending too much time with Mr. Sullivan—he's starting to rub off on me. If I ever push you too far, just let me know."

"Of course, sir. You don't, sir." Westward took in a warbling breath. "But, please, no matter if you're pregnant or not—"

I definitely was.

"—don't go in the office just yet. Lena will be out in a second with the mop. I don't want any workplace accidents."

"It's just a little spilled water," I objected. "I'll be careful now that I know what to look out for."

"No!" It was very rare for Westward to raise his voice, and

it startled me enough to stop me from circling around him and continuing on my way.

I squinted at him. Something suspicious was going on, but it was impossible to tell what. "Did Mr. Sullivan cause trouble with something while I was gone?" I asked. "Or is this about the visitor? As far as I'm aware, we had no appointments scheduled for today."

"No, no, no, no." Westward shook his head harder than before. "It's water, sir. Spilled water. Very dangerous, wet, slippery water. Please let Lena finish mopping it up before you go inside. It's all over the floor, sir. Very bad news. You'll go in and instantly slip—or worse, you'll hit Lena with the door and push her to the floor and she'll get soaking wet. You'll never hear the end of it then."

I held back a laugh—Westward was right about that. Five months later, Lena still had the squirt bottle on her desk in case I got out of control. I was honestly surprised it had taken as long as it had for it to get knocked down and spilled. I supposed, all things considered, I could wait. Another five minutes wasn't going to kill me. "Okay, Westward. You win. I'll wait."

Westward's shoulders slumped in relief. Beaming, he wiped his brow and looked over his shoulder at the door. On cue, it opened, and Lena wheeled out a yellow mop bucket. I was shocked—I'd thought for sure that West-ward had been telling tall tales on Troy's behalf.

Go figure.

"Hello, Mr. Mills," Lena said flatly as she rolled the mop bucket down the hall. "The water's all cleaned up. The office is safe to walk through again."

"Oh, thank god," Westward uttered, much more enthused than he should have been over the state of the floor.

I looked between him and Lena, my eyes narrowed suspiciously. "Did I go out for a lunchtime milkshake and walk back into an alternate dimension? Something weird is going on."

"Nothing's weird!" Westward insisted a little too eagerly. He wrung his hands like something was *very* weird. "Everything's fine. I was waiting to go see Mr. Sullivan, so let's go to the office together."

I looked back and forth between Lena and Westward, but ended up following Westward down the hall. Lena continued on her way, pushing the mop bucket back to the janitorial closet.

"This is the part where you knock me out and steal one of my kidneys, isn't it?" I asked as Westward opened the door to reception. I didn't see any sign that water had been spilled on the floor. "Or is it a lung you're after? Maybe both? A section of my liver? My mother had cancer, you know. Bile duct cancer. She had to go through several rounds of neoadjuvant chemo, and then a partial hepatectomy. Those are big scary words, right? Hopefully enough to convince you that my organs aren't prime real estate for the black market?"

"Mr. Mills," Westward said pointedly. "If I'd wanted to harvest your organs, I would have done so a long time ago. I think it's safe to say you're in the clear."

I hadn't been expecting Westward to joke back, and as a consequence, I burst out laughing. I was still in stitches when I set my hand on the exterior doorknob of the office door. Lena's desk was no more than a few feet away—the spray bottle was gone. "Westward? Never change. You're incredible."

"I try, sir," Westward assured me. He waved a hand at the door. "Now, go on. I don't have all day to wait outside. There's business to tend to."

"Yes, yes." I pulled myself together and opened the door. It took me two steps to realize that the office I'd left half an hour ago wasn't the one I returned to now. Stunned, I stopped and stared. Three dozen roses lay on Troy's office

MASTER WANTED | 215

desk, dark red and in full bloom. Accented by white baby's breath, they were absolutely gorgeous. Troy, always prim and proper, looked even more phenomenally handsome than the last time I'd seen him—he'd changed into a richer suit and swapped out his tie for one with a color that made his eyes pop. But, of all those things, the one that surprised me the most was the visitor standing to the side of Troy's desk.

Mom.

"Hi, baby," Mom said with a wink and a smile. Her hair had grown into a short, shaggy hairdo that framed her cheekbones beautifully. If I hadn't known she'd been so sick just a year ago, I never would have believed it. "You're all glowy. Pregnancy suits you."

"Mom?" I rushed into the room, too overcome with joy to think about Troy or the roses. I tugged Mom into a hug, and she laughed and hugged me back. "Mom, what are you doing here? I thought you wanted to stay in Maine."

"Troy invited me to come visit," she said. She pulled away from me and grinned, love shining in her eyes. "He's a lovely man. I'm glad that you've found each other."

"I just... I can't get over this!" I laughed. I'd tried to convince Mom to come down and visit since I'd flown out to Las Vegas, but she always had some excuse or another. I had no idea how Troy had managed to get her out of Rock-port. "Does Monty know you're here? Where is he?"

"He was out of town on business today," Troy told me. He was smiling ear to ear. "I'd asked him to be here, too, but he couldn't change his plans around. He sends his love."

I turned my attention from Mom to Troy, confused. "Here for what...?"

Troy stepped around his desk, our eyes locked. Over the last few months, his confidence had blossomed, and I loved to see him be so bold.

I was so distracted by the look in his eyes that I didn't realize what was happening until he dropped to one knee. My eyes widened, and I pinched my shoulder blades together as my whole body tensed.

"For the day I ask you to be mine forever," Troy said. From his inner suit pocket, he produced a ring box. He pulled back the top to reveal a simple band inside—plat-inum with a small, black stone set flush with the surface of the ring. "Will you marry me, Robin, and make our small family official?"

An answer launched itself from my mouth before I could even think about it. I had no doubt or hesitation, and I felt no regret. I knew what I wanted, and what I wanted was Troy. "*Yes!*"

Flashes went off behind me—someone was taking pictures. Westward and Lena *had* been scamming. They'd followed me back into the office so they could capture the big moment for me and Troy.

I brushed tears away from my eyes. It was *totally* the pregnancy making me emotional. Yep. It definitely wasn't like I was tearing up over my stubborn, big-headed, absolutely wonderful man.

"I love you, Robin," Troy whispered as he slipped the ring on my finger and stood, drawing me into his arms. "I love you for you."

"I love you, too." I rested my head on his shoulder, then laughed. When I spoke again, I whispered what I had to say into his ear. "But you know, this ring wasn't an approved purchase... and neither were those flowers. Even if they were for me, that doesn't forgive the fact that you didn't ask for permission."

Troy shivered. My grin grew.

"I think, later tonight, I might have to punish you for what you've done."

"You two remind me of what me and my late husband were like when we were younger," Mom enthused from much closer than I'd previously believed. I jumped back, cheeks red—she'd definitely heard us. "Back then, when he misbehaved, I would—"

"Oh my god, Mom!" I uttered, exasperated. "*Really?*"

Mom winked. "You're a Mills, Robin. It's in our genes."

24

TROY

That night, after dinner with Mrs. Mills and promises to visit the tourist traps the next day, Robin took me home to our estate and let Master out to play. With cool, unwavering confidence, he marched me past my bodyguard, Damien, who'd given me resources on where to find the best engagement rings, and to our bedroom, where he closed the door, but didn't draw the curtains. Tiny, solar-powered garden lights illuminated sections of the property outside my floor-to-ceiling windows, drawing the eye to the multi-level rock gardens in the distance, and the lush, green grass that our gardening staff took great care in protecting from the harsh climate.

"You're been a bad boy lately, haven't you, Troy?" Master

asked as he moved toward the bathroom door. I watched him go, enchanted. Since we'd had our conversation after finding out about Robin's pregnancy, Master had come out to play very rarely—we'd ended our contract and instead let play happen when it did. I was happy with that arrangement, and I think Robin was, too. It gave him the freedom he wanted to turn to me for strength without worrying that I'd lose interest or see him as weak.

He came to a stop in the bathroom doorway. "You may speak."

"I have been bad, Master," I replied. My heart slammed against my rib cage, and my pulse rushed in my ears. I was already starting to get hard, and all Master had done was speak to me.

"So naughty." Master clucked his tongue. "We're going to have to do something about that. While I'm busy in the bathroom, I want you to strip. When I come out again, I want you completely naked, spread across the bed, and ready for me. Do you understand?"

"Yes, Master." My cock stood at attention, pushing against the front of my slacks. I wanted out of them in the worst way, but I figured Master would only want me to strip once he was out of the room. Until then, I'd have to stand at attention.

A pleased look crossed Master's face. He laid a hand on the wood lining of the doorframe, then shot me a tiny smirk that sent all my blood south. It was the kind of look that said that the punishment I was about to receive would please us both. "Good. Then I expect to find you naked and on the bed by the time I get back."

Master locked himself in the bathroom, and I sprang into action. I rushed to loosen my tie and shrug off my jacket, then undid my shirt button by button. I hopped across the room to the closet as I pulled off my shoes and socks, then pulled my belt open and yanked down my pants. I stepped out of my boxers, tossed the mess into the hamper to deal with later—even the pieces of my suit which should have been hung—and hurried back to the bed. Completely nude, I crawled across the mattress and sank down amongst the soft sheets. My head rested on the pillows. Since Master had moved in, and especially now that his pregnancy was starting to become more burdensome, the number of pillows on our bed had increased by a significant amount.

I lay still while my chest rose and fell heavily, my lungs desperate to suck in as much air as they could. My heart seemed to have convinced my body that I was running a race, and I was winded with excitement. While I waited, I closed my eyes and imagined all the things that Master might do to punish me for spending money on frivolous things without his permission—even though those frivolous things had been for him. Maybe he'd put weights around my balls and force me to wear them while we stood in front of the open window, exposing myself to the world. Maybe he'd force me to blow him until he came and demand I hold his cum in my mouth while he inserted it one fingerful at a time into my ass, then seal it up with a plug and make me sleep like that. Maybe—

The bathroom door opened, and Master returned. He'd changed into a black silk robe, his legs and feet bare. The robe was tied at the front just over the small bump of his belly, emphasizing it. As soon as I looked over, I couldn't help but stare. The wicked gleam in his eyes and the sleek, black silk lent him power and sophistication. Even pregnant, he knew that he was in control, and he wasn't afraid to get what he wanted.

I spotted my ring on his finger, the platinum beautiful against the color of his skin. I had a feeling that no matter how much time passed, I would never tire of seeing him wear it.

"I see you're trying very hard to make it up to me," he told me as he reached the bedside. "You're going to have to try just a little harder. Since we met, you've been disobedient quite a few times, haven't you? I feel like, if you want to apologize, you'll need to prove you really are sorry..."

As he spoke, he observed me. His hungry eyes moved down my chest to my navel, then to my hardened cock. With a tilt of his head and a flash of his eyes, his gaze returned to my face.

"Roll over, Troy. I want you on your knees."

The command arrowed through me, and I wasted no time rolling over so I could lift myself up on my hands and knees. I heard silk pool on the floor by the side of the bed, then heard as Master drew something out of our toy chest stowed in the storage space beneath the bedframe. Wood clicked against wood. Metal slid. The mattress dipped. Master's soft hand traced over the curve of my ass, then dipped between my legs until his fingers toyed with my balls. I sucked in a breath and tried not to tremble, but it was impossible. I'd already let go of the hard realities of life to slip into subspace, and now that I was there, I couldn't get over how every little thing he did was for my benefit. The more I gave myself to him, mind, body, and soul, the more he gave back to me. We were caught in an endless feedback loop of pleasure, and it was easy to imagine that it would last forever.

"Stay still," Master said. His hand closed around my balls,

pulling my skin taut as he guided them back between my legs. A smooth, wooden surface caressed my thighs, tucking itself right below the curve of my ass. Master brought my balls over it, then clamped a second wooden piece in place over them, securing my balls in place without pinching them. There was discomfort, but not pain. "Do you know what I'm doing to you, Troy? You may speak."

"No, Master," I replied. Whatever it was, it was turning me on. The way it pulled my balls taut made sure that I stayed alert and kept still, because the more I moved and stretched my legs, the more I'd stretch my balls.

Master chuckled. It was a sinful sound, and it shot right through me. I shivered again, sending pinpricks of pain through my balls and groin. His hands traced along the backs of my thighs, then up along my ass.

"This, Troy," he whispered, "is a humbler. It'll keep your balls stretched and hold them back between your legs, forcing you to stay on your hands and knees. The more you move, the more pain you'll feel. You might consider it an incentive to make sure you stay on your best behavior."

Master smacked my ass just then, the sound more startling than the crisp pain that seared my ass. I jolted forward, and just like Master had warned me, the humbler remained in place, holding my balls back. Pain radiated through my groin and into my stomach, and with a pained moan, I returned to position.

Master rubbed where he'd smacked apologetically. "Count for me, Troy. Count every spank I give you, and thank me for being strong enough to correct you, even when you're bad."

Even with the receding pain in my balls, arousal surged through me. All of my blood had rushed south, and my cock pulsed. A thin strand of precum leaked from my tip and dangled, a precursor of what was to come. I *wanted* this. My brave, strong, wonderful Master was confident enough to run a company by day and dominate me in the bedroom by night. He ruled the world, and while he did, he ruled *my* world.

Everything I did, I did for him, and I knew he did the same for me.

"One," I uttered. My heart hammered, and my tongue was so drunk with need, it almost stumbled over the syllables. "Thank you, Master."

Another sharp slap, this time to the opposite cheek. I tried my best to hold back, but in the end, I lurched forward just a little. Trembling with arousal, barely feeling the pain, I corrected my position to ease the tension on my balls. "T-Two. Thank you, Master."

Smack.

"*Three.*" The strand of precum snapped. With my head hung, I was able to watch it hit the sheets and disappear. A new bead of it, clear and glistening, had started to collect where the strand had hung. "Thank you, Master."

Smack!

My ass was hot, but the synapses in my brain were confused. All I felt was pleasure.

With a cry that turned into a moan, I announced, "*Four!* Thank you, Master."

The fifth, sixth, and seventh spanks came in rapid succession. By then, my tongue was tied and I could barely speak, I was moaning so much. My balls ached, my cock was painfully hard, and my body wanted nothing more than to thrust into a tight, wet hole and shoot my seed. The eighth and ninth spanks left me dizzy and flying high, and I made sounds I hoped turned into words, but the tenth spank sent me to astronomical heights. With a primal cry, I bucked forward, realized my mistake, and trembled and shook as I tried to fight my instincts to breed. I wanted claim Master's tight body while I buried my nose in the crook of his neck and scented him. I wanted to draw the fragrance of his omega into my lungs and never let it go. I wanted to bring him to orgasm over and over again, and come in him in turn. If he weren't already pregnant, I would have given him a baby tonight. I couldn't resist him. I needed him more than I needed air—he was my everything.

"Good boy, Troy," Master praised after I'd counted and thanked him for the tenth spank. He moved around from behind me, and my eyes widened. I'd believed Master to be naked beneath his robe, but that wasn't the case. A pretty pair of red lace panties with ribbons crisscrossed over the front panel hugged his dick, stretched slightly by his pregnant belly. My dick throbbed. They were the same panties I'd bought him months ago—the ones he'd pulled from his back pocket upon first meeting me to confirm his identity.

Even pregnant, he looked flawless in them, his cock hugged by the fabric just like I thought it'd be.

He made eye contact with me, then slipped them off and surprised me by bending over to pick something out of our chest of toys. When he'd grabbed it, he slipped between my arms and body and looked directly up at me. In his hand, he held a purple jelly dildo. "You deserve a little break, I think. Why don't you rest and recover while I take care of myself, hmm?"

My eyes widened. *What?*

Lust in his eyes, Master bit down on his lip and slipped the dildo between his legs. On my knees, with my head hanging, I was able to watch as he shifted his hips back and forth, then slid the toy inside himself. He moaned the tiniest, sweetest moan I'd ever heard, then started to pump the dildo in and out as he moved his hips to meet each movement.

There had never been a more exquisite torture.

I wanted to be inside him. I wanted to be the cock buried in his ass, pushing against his prostate and pushing him toward orgasm. I wanted to fucking tear that dildo out of him, throw it across the room, and show him how he *deserved* to be fucked.

"Oh, fuck," Master whispered under his breath. He arched his back and then bore down on the dildo, putting on a show. "*Fuck,* feels good... feels so fucking good..."

My hips had started to pump, and even though they didn't move far, pain spiked through my balls and reminded me that I was under Master's control. Until he released me, I had to be good. I had to listen and obey, no matter how hard it was. Tears of frustration pooled in my eyes, and I gritted my teeth.

"It's hitting my prostate." Master moaned. "It's hitting my prostate, Troy. Oh, *fuck!* Gonna make me come... it's gonna make me come!"

I wanted to shout, to scream, to convince him to stop so that I could finish the job, but I knew that wasn't my place. All I could do was watch as Master rode the dildo beneath me, so close we touched, but far enough away that I'd never be able to do what I wanted to do the most. It was a reminder that he was the one calling the shots— that I was to listen and to serve, no matter what. What Master wanted, he would get. That was the way I always wanted it to be.

I waited for him to go rigid and come, but that moment never arrived. With a breathy sigh, he pulled the dildo out and tossed it aside, then climbed out from beneath me and returned behind me again. Metal twisted on itself, and all of a sudden, the polished wood holding my balls back released. The tension disappeared, and Master took the toy away.

I was free.

"Throw me on the fucking bed and *fuck me*, Troy,"

Master said from behind me. He tossed the wooden humbler to the floor, where it clacked, then was forgotten. "Take me like the fucking animal I've turned you into."

I *was* an animal. Seeing Master play with that dildo had lit a fire inside of me that refused to be extinguished. My vision blurred at the edges and sharpened in the center, and I lunged, pinning Master to the edge of the bed. He squeaked in delight and spread his thighs, and seconds later, I'd yanked him into position and pushed inside of him, driving my cock home again and again.

"F-f-fuck!" Master panted. He grabbed at my neck, holding himself steady. I snarled and claimed his lips in a savage kiss, pushing into him over and over again. The tightness of his body gripped me, and whatever he'd used to prepare himself while in the bathroom let our bodies glide together effortlessly. My leaking cock had found its home, and now, it wasn't going to leave.

"Come in me," Master demanded when our lips parted. He met each of my hurried thrusts with wiggles of his hips, driving me deeper and increasing my pleasure. "Fucking come in me, Troy. I want it. I want to *feel you*."

I was his to command. With a roar, I pushed forward and emptied into him, shooting again and again. Master went rigid, and his passage tightened around my throbbing cock. I bucked into him a few more times, then fell still. Panting, I claimed his lips in a shorter, gentler kiss as I came down from my high.

"I love you, Troy." Robin spoke this time. He wove his hands through my hair and caressed my scalp, the softened smile on his face entirely satisfied. He'd come when I had, and it seemed like he was coming down right beside me. "I love you like crazy."

"I love you, too." I pulled out slowly and lay beside him, drawing him into my arms. "I love you so much. Thank you for looking after me like you do."

Robin snorted. He buried his face against my chest. "It goes two ways, you know. Thank you for what you do for me. Thank you for respecting me, for believing in me, for sticking by me, even when I'm a lunatic..."

"I'm a stubborn asshole, so it all works out." I kissed the top of his head. "I don't think you're a lunatic, you know."

"You will after spending some time with my mom." Robin laughed. "But you know what? If you can survive a Mills family reunion, I think everything's going to be okay. This baby's going to be half Mills, you know. Work oriented, kinky as fuck, and—"

"Incredibly talented?" I asked, grinning. "Highly intelligent? The embodiment of perfection?"

"Crazy," he concluded. "But, I mean, since he's taking after you, he *might* be those things, too."

God, did I love him. I kissed him all over again, and soon enough, I was back inside of him, making love to the man that would one day be my husband.

25

TROY

On a sweltering June morning, Robin shook me from a deep sleep. I blinked the sleep from my eyes and looked up at him to find the lights were already on, and he was fully dressed. It had to be close to four—our alarm wasn't set to go off for another hour and a half, at least.

"Robin?" I asked, groggy.

"Get out of bed, Troy," Master demanded. He spoke with total calmness and clarity. "The baby is coming, and you need to take me to the hospital."

I snapped awake in an instant and threw back the covers. Master stood at the bedside, an overnight bag already slung over his shoulder. At nine months pregnant, he was big, but I found him more beautiful than ever. With glowing, radiant skin and effortless paternal instinct, every day he aspired toward divinity. And right now, the life he'd devoted himself to creating was ready to meet the world for the first time.

What was I supposed to do?

We'd come up with a plan, but all I could remember was the end goal: get Robin to the hospital. There were other steps, other things I needed to remember. What were we supposed to bring? What was the drop-off point? Who was I supposed to call?

"Troy." Master cupped my face with both his hands, holding me still until I focused on him. We looked at each other eye to eye. His calming, dominant disposition put me at ease and helped clear my panic away. "Calm down. It's okay. All you need to do is get me to the hospital—I've taken care of the rest."

"Okay," I whispered. I wasn't sure if I was allowed to speak, but it seemed important that I make it known that I had understood.

"The car should be ready, right?" Master asked. "Do you want to drive, or do you want to be driven? You'll need to call your driver if you want to be driven."

"I'll call him." My phone was charging on my bedside table, and I reached for it. I was stripped down to my boxers, but the minute it would take me to throw on a shirt, pants, and shoes would be all it would take for the car to be brought out front. While I tended to that, Master went to stand by the door. He looked down the hall, then back at me. I thought I saw him wince.

"Are you okay?" I asked as I hopped on one foot, pulling on a sock.

Robin was back now, his expression flat and unimpressed. He raised an eyebrow. "Troy? I don't know if you've been made aware, but I'm in labor and about to have a baby. Do you want to rethink that question?"

I finished putting on my socks and grabbed my shoes, hopping across the bedroom floor toward the door as I put them on. "I... yes. I'm just... it's a lot to process."

"It is." All the while, Robin kept his voice level. I didn't know how he could be so composed in the face of hours of physically taxing pain. "Now, let's get going. If we can avoid it, I'd prefer not to have our baby in the back seat of the car."

"Right." Robin needed me, and I was going to be there for him. If that meant unscrambling my brains and putting my head on straight, I'd figure out a way to do it. "I've got this under control. I'm ready to go."

"Um... Troy?" Robin pushed his lips to the side, holding back a smirk. "Your shoe." He pointed at the shoe I was still holding—the one I'd already forgotten about. "You might want to put that on before we go."

My face flooded with heat, and I bobbed my head in agreement. "I... I was going to get to that in a second."

Robin chuckled and shook his head, but when he looked at me, his face was full of so much love that my heart sang. "You're something else, Troy. I hope that even after we become fathers and grow old—or *older*—together, that we'll still be like this."

"We will," I promised as I put on my shoe. "We might change, but as long as we're together, I don't think we have anything to worry about."

"You sap." He ran a hand over his low-hanging stomach, then looked my way and smiled. "You're going to make a good dad, you know that?"

Shoe finally on, I put both feet on the floor. "I won't be the only one."

"Ugh. Now I'm diabetic *and* pregnant. Great." Robin's

grin was all I needed to put my head back on straight. "I'll meet you at the car."

"No, I'll go with you." I stood and took his hand. He flashed me a smile that was worth more than all my millions of dollars in investments and the cash I kept in my accounts.

Whatever it took, and wherever the journey led us, I would be at his side. There was no alternative.

SIX HOURS OF LABOR LATER, a sweaty and exhausted Robin cried out through his teeth and pushed one final time. The thin sheet provided by the hospital lay crumpled on the floor, and Robin's hospital gown was half ripped from his body. I watched, astounded and overwhelmed, as a dark head of hair crowned, and our obstetrician pulled our newborn free.

There was a frightening minute where there was no noise. The baby was a dark red color that I wasn't sure was natural. Breath held, I took a step toward the doctor and my child and was about to ask what was wrong when the baby sucked in a breath and started to wail. Robin, who'd slumped back onto the hospital bed, folded an arm over his eyes and drew in a rattling breath almost in tandem.

"Congratulations," our obstetrician said. He smiled at me as he handed our child off to the attending nurse. "It's a boy."

A boy. I grinned, then went to stand by Robin's side and took his hand. He unfolded his arm from over his eyes and looked up at me. Although he was exhausted, I saw how proud he was of what he'd just done—of what we'd done together.

"A boy," Robin said, astonished. "You know, statistically, I shouldn't be surprised. You're more likely to have a male child if you conceive with an older partner."

"Is that a jab?" I asked.

Robin shrugged a single shoulder. He should have been too tired to joke, but he powered through regardless. "Depends on if you take getting old personally, old man."

I held back a laugh and kissed the top of his sweat-soaked head.

"What's his name?" the nurse asked as she brought the baby back. He'd been lightly cleaned, and while she carried him wrapped in a blanket, he wasn't swaddled.

When she placed him on Robin's chest, they made skin-to-skin contact. In that moment, I saw Robin melt. A mellow adoration washed over him, and all of his exhaustion and worry melted away. He held our child, and as he did, I fell in love with them both. My family—my forever. My heart had never been so full.

"Spencer," Robin said with finality. It was the name of his father—a man he sorely missed. "Spencer Sullivan. Happy birthday, little man. Your dads love you very much already."

Spencer settled as he snuggled with Robin, and Robin settled, too. I sat at the bedside and held him loosely, my eyes closed and a perpetual smile on my face. There were moments in life that would drag me down and wear me out, but right now, with my new family, I felt like nothing would hit me quite as hard anymore. In them, I'd found purpose and inspiration. Even if it took every cent I had, I would cherish and protect them. I'd found love, and I would submit to it forever.

EPILOGUE

"I suppose this means you're retiring." Monty held Spencer to his chest, cradling him slowly back and forth while Spencer slept. Mom, who'd flown down to welcome Spencer into the world, was asleep in the next room, jet lagged. Since I wasn't living in the condo anymore, we'd decided to use it as a guest house for Mom, and we'd met there today for dinner. Troy had stayed home to sleep a little, although I wasn't sure why. The horrors I'd heard about newborns weren't true— Spencer didn't cry all the time. He slept, and ate, and slept, then pooped, and slept and ate some more. Well, maybe there was a little more pooping. To be honest, I tried to block that out.

I guess being older than me didn't help Troy's case. My body was ready to bounce back, but his was more set in its ways. Hopefully, in the next little while, he'd get it figured out—Mom had been gracious enough to inform me that once Spencer reached two years old, all bets were off. Unholy terror would unleash itself upon our household, and we'd feel run ragged at the best of times.

I was ready, and I expected Troy to bring his A game as well. If not, there would be consequences.

I smirked.

God, did I love that man. I'd been reluctant to come out to dinner tonight without him, but now I had our reunion to look forward to. We didn't spend much time apart these days, and that was the way I liked it. My stubborn, pigheaded soon-to-be-husband was someone I couldn't get enough of, and in everything he said and did, I knew the sentiment went both ways.

"I am," I replied at last. "Not that I was doing any work for you, anyway. Troy was my one-and-done."

"Is Spencer?"

I looked to the side and smiled. Was it weird to have baby fever after just having a baby? Yeah, probably. It didn't stop me, though. The thought of having more children with Troy appealed to me an insane amount. The feelings I got when I saw him hold Spencer close and kiss his forehead were second to none, and I could easily imagine in the future, when Spencer was older, how I'd melt while Troy snuggled up to a toddler with our newborn son or daughter in his arms.

"I'll take that as a no," Monty said in good humor. He looked down at Spencer with adoration. "I don't mind being an uncle several times over. You and Troy make cute children. Who would have thought?"

"Who would have thought indeed." I cuddled back against the couch, getting comfy while thoughts of Troy threatened to distract me. "I'll have you know that I'm not full-on retiring, by the way. I'm still going to be working in the executive offices of The Palisade, keeping an eye on Troy. He's done a fine job unlearning all his archaic business habits, but I think he can do better. If you'd like, once I get a handle on being a dad and a professional, I'd love to come back to Rent-a-Dom, too, as an executive, of course. I feel like I've got a new perspective, now that I've put in some time at the casino. You think you can handle me?"

"Me?" Monty chuckled. "I don't know, little brother—you're in the big leagues now. I'm not sure I can keep up."

I held back a laugh. "Then I'll whip you into shape. I'm qualified."

"Fat chance." Monty touched a finger very lightly to Spencer's nose. "Besides, you said it yourself—you're retiring. The only one on the receiving end of your whip is going to be your husband-to-be. Poor submissive alphas everywhere weep."

"Shut up." If he hadn't been holding Spencer, I would have elbowed him. "It's not that big a deal. I landed you a whopping one contract. I'm not exactly a career Dom. Besides, like I said, I'd only be going back in at an executive level. I am *not* open to taking any more contracts. It doesn't matter who the sub is."

Monty's question did, however, prompt my mind to wander. Retirement, families, babies...

"Do you have plans to retire soon?" I asked, making it totally transparent that I was prodding him. "You've been away on business trips a lot, taking on at least one client that I know of..."

Monty shot me a look that would have killed a stone. "No."

"I think the lady doth—"

"No," he stated again. Then, in his usual wise, musing tone, said, "Not for a while. There are too many things I want to see and do before I think about 'retiring.'"

"So no chance at a cousin for Spencer to grow up with?"

More stones died. "Robin."

I snorted. While his Dom voice was all the right kinds of intimidating, it was too close to my own to take seriously.

"I'm done, I'm done." I waved him off. "I'm just giving you a hard time."

"I know. And really? I'm glad for it. It means that you're home again—that we're back in the same place, at the same time." Monty smiled. "No more phone conversations."

"No more tape over your webcam," I added.

Monty shrugged. "I mean, the tape is still there, but you don't have to worry about it anymore."

"You're so paranoid."

"And you're not careful enough." Monty shook his head. "But that's neither here nor there. The illusion stands, and that's what's important. This year is Rent-a-Dom's fourth anniversary—can you believe it? Next year will be the big half-decade mark."

"Has it really been that long?" I scrunched my nose. "It feels like it hasn't been any time at all."

"I know. I'm still trying to decide what we should do about it." Monty grinned, looking down at Spencer. "Wouldn't it be something to hold a birthday party?"

I held back a laugh. "Pin the butt plug on the sub?"

Monty nodded. "You don't want to know what I have planned for the piñata."

I choked back a laugh, both for Mom's sake, and for Spencer's.

"But for now," Monty said, "I'm just happy all of us are together again. You, me, Mom, Spencer, and now Troy. It feels right somehow—like the world isn't so wide and scary."

"We made it, Monty." I took Spencer from him, holding my son to my chest. He shifted in his sleep and made small smacking sounds with his lips. Everything he did was so stinking cute I could barely take it. "We beat the odds."

"And we're going to keep winning," Monty promised. "I know it."

I grinned and caught his eye, identical to my own in every way.

"Of course we are," I said. "We're Mills—it's in our genes."

STAY IN TOUCH

What happens when your fated mate is also your natural predator?
Join Susi Hawke's mailing list and get your FREE copy of The Rabbit Chase

Can't get enough omegaverse?
Join Piper Scott's mailing list and get your FREE copy of the oh, so sexy Yes, Professor

Find Susi Hawke on Facebook:
https://www.facebook.com/susihawkeauthor

Find Piper Scott on Facebook:
https://www.facebook.com/groups/PiperScott

ALSO BY SUSI HAWKE

Northern Lodge Pack Series

Northern Pines Den Series

Blood Legacy Chronicles

The Hollydale Omegas

MacIntosh Meadows Series

Lone Star Brothers Series

Three Hearts Collection
(with Harper B. Cole)

Team A.L.P.H.A Series
(with Crista Crown)

Waking the Dragon Series
(with Piper Scott)

Rent-a-Dom Series

(with Piper Scott)

ALSO BY PIPER SCOTT

Rutledge Triplets Series

His Command Series

Single Dad Support Group Series

Waking the Dragon Series
(with Susi Hawke)

Rent-a-Dom Series
(with Susi Hawke)

CPSIA information can be obtained
at www.ICGtesting.com
Printed in the USA
LVHW112335040119
602856LV00001B/83/P

9 781720 255864